BAD BOY

AT SCHOOL

Thanks for putting up with us!

Lots a love

Sue Ritter
xx

[signature]

BAD BOY AT SCHOOL

SUE RITTER

WORD PUBLISHING

Word (UK) Ltd
Milton Keynes, England

WORD AUSTRALIA
Heathmont, Victoria, Australia
SUNDAY SCHOOL CENTRE WHOLESALE
Salt River, South Africa
ALBY COMMERCIAL ENTERPRISES PTE LTD
Balmoral Road, Singapore
CONCORDE DISTRIBUTORS LTD
Havelock North, New Zealand
CROSS (HK) CO
Hong Kong

BAD BOY AT SCHOOL

Contents

There are a lot of kids who will recognise themselves in this book. Although it has not been written about real characters, I'd like to dedicate it to the kids of "Royal Week" and "Young Harvest". They know who they are! Enjoy it!

1

One of those Nights

"I'll get it!"

The phone in Terry's house is under the stairs. It's not exactly the most private place in the world — especially if you get a phone call from someone you fancy … as it happened this one wasn't, it was just from Martin, one of his mates.

"Oh hi, Martin, it's you."

"Course it's me!" said Martin. "Why, who were you expecting, eh?"

"I wasn't expecting anyone much, I just wondered, that's all," replied Terry.

"Tracey! You thought it was Tracey, didn't you? Come on, own up, Tell!"

"Look," Terry interrupted, "What did you phone for anyway?"

"Ha! You *did* think it was Tracey! Have you asked her out yet? It's about time you know, everyone knows she fancies you!" replied Martin, enjoying himself.

"As a matter of fact, I wasn't expecting any phone call from anyone, least of all her! Martin, be a good lad and tell me what you want," said Terry patiently.

"Oh, nothing much really. I've just bought a couple

of new albums and my mum and dad have gone out and left me in charge of the stereo. Want to come over?"

"Well, as it happens I've just finished my homework. You didn't get that Dire Straits LP, did you?" asked Terry, wondering whether the Lord agreed with the copyright laws about taping other people's records.

"That'll depend on whether you'll help me with my homework. If you will, I think I can guarantee that one of the new albums is in fact Dire Straits. So you're going to come over, then?" laughed Martin.

"Yeh, give me half an hour," replied Terry.

"See you then."

"Bye." Terry put the phone down, grinned, and went to find an empty cassette tape.

"Finished with the phone, Terry?" asked Mrs. Ellis.

"Yeh, all done," he replied.

"There's a love. I'm giving Mrs. Myers a ring, we've got that committee meeting down at church to discuss meeting in houses during the week." Mrs. Ellis always looked confident when she discussed church matters. Her heart was in the right place when it came to being a Christian, but there was nothing she liked better than a committee meeting. "I expect the vicar will have a lot to say about that, I wonder whose houses they'll use?"

"A meeting to discuss a meeting? Well, when you've sorted it out let me know the outcome, OK?" smiled Terry. He got on well with his mum, even if she did tend to treat him a bit too much like 'her little boy'. She believed in indulging her children while they were still at home.

Carol wandered into the room, carrying a magazine in one hand and an apple in the other. Carol, Terry's sister, could never do one thing at a time. She got bored very quickly, so her ideal in life would be to read a book whilst having one eye on the TV, with a packet of crisps at her side (to give her something to do with her hands) and the family dog on her lap.

"Who was that?" she enquired.

"Who was what?" asked Terry knowing full well what she meant, but enjoying the tease.

"On the phone," said Carol. "Who was it?"

"Only Martin," replied Terry.

"What do you mean, *only* Martin, were you expecting someone else? Not that Tracey! Honestly, Tell, she's got you wrapped round her finger and she's really not your type." Carol spoke confidently with all the knowledge and wisdom of a fourteen year old girl. Besides, she'd lined her brother up for her best mate Sharon, who might not look quite as good as Tracey — but then, who liked Tracey?

"Oh don't *you* start! I promise you it was Martin who phoned, and it is Martin I am going round to see and when I get there, it is Martin's album we are going to listen to." 'And there I rest my case,' thought Terry.

"Can I come?"

"'Fraid not, Caz. Anyway, George Michael doesn't sing in Dire Straits, so you wouldn't be interested." Terry picked up his jacket and rubbed a mark off the sleeve. "We also have to discuss the school Christian Union," he said casually.

"Oh, right, well I'd better not come then." Already losing interest, Carol turned her attention to the apple and then the magazine.

'Ha!' thought Terry. 'I thought that would work! Sorry, Lord, I know it's mean but I didn't really want her along.'

The mirror in the hall told Terry that he looked great, even though he hadn't worked on it. Most people could work on their appearance for a week and never come up with that much style.

"See you later," Terry yelled as he closed the front door.

It was cold outside. September was a dodgy month, you never knew whether to take a jacket, just wear a sweater or put a coat on. Tonight Terry wished he'd put a coat on. Turning up his collar he strolled towards the bus stop and as he did, the bus went sailing past him! There was no point in waiting in the cold for fifteen minutes for the next one — it would only take fifteen minutes to walk through town. "Ah well, God made legs before man made buses," sighed Terry, not totally convinced of the logic behind his remark.

Meanwhile, on the other side of the town, there were no phone calls for Bob Harris. Mainly because there was no phone in his house, and even if there was, he wasn't exactly the most popular fella in Brenton. Bob was what is generally termed — a rebel (that's if you're being generous) and rebels don't normally have friends, they have sort of followers and people who just stare at them from a distance.

The fact that Bob didn't have any definite mates was a real pain, because he didn't have much of a family life either. There was only him and his dad at home; his mum left when he was about eight and he had never really decided whether he would never forgive her — or whether he'd give his right arm for her to come home again.

Anyway, all this had made Bob a pretty hard sort of character. He was a mixture of someone who threw bricks through shop windows for no reason and some-one who had to go home from school every night and try and sober his old man up enough to give him the dinner that *he* had to prepare for him. It wasn't much of an existence, but it was the only one he knew.

To look at him, you would find yourself combing the scruffy locks, mending the holes in his tee shirt, giving him a smile instead of that permanent frown — and finding an almost good-looking, fair haired, nearly-six-teen year old bloke. Not that he ever saw that for him-self, because there was nobody at home (or at school for that matter) who would give him the chance to find out.

His dad had given up on life. When his wife walked out on him, he picked up a bottle of scotch and had been drowning his sorrows ever since. To him, his son was just a nuisance. Bobby Harris was in the way and lately there'd been trouble at school and his name was always first on the list of troublemakers.

Right now, Mr. Harris was slumped in his usual armchair staring blankly at the telly.

"Oi, Bob!" he yelled.

Bob was sitting in the kitchen reading a magazine about motorbikes. He slammed the mag on the table and wandered into the front room.

"What?" he asked without enthusiasm.

"Get your dad a nice cuppa tea, eh?" said Mr. Harris without looking up.

"Get it yourself!" replied Bob and promptly went back into the kitchen.

"Bob! Get your carcase in 'ere!" yelled his dad. He was grumpy now; it hadn't been a very good day for him, he'd lost on the dogs and there was nothing on TV.

Bob strolled in and faced his dad. "Look," he said, "I've been at school all day, I've cooked your tea, washed up and I think I deserve some time off for good behaviour." He started to go...

"Tea, I said!" growled Mr. Harris.

And now Bob wasn't in a very good mood either.

"Get it yourself, I'm off out!" he yelled, whipped his jacket off the chair and went out, slamming the door behind him.

It was one of those nights when you can't find anybody. All the regular places seemed to be empty and the space by the benches in the walkabout part of town was pretty vacant too, apart from a couple of kids spinning on their heads to the sound of a record going backwards. 'Stupid idiots,' thought Bob, and tripped the little fella up. Before he could retaliate Bob had flung him out of the way and proceeded to show him how breakdancing *should* be done! It wasn't that he particularly liked breakdancing ... it was just that he was bored and liked to show off a bit. The music ended abruptly as the two kids picked up their ghetto blaster and belted up the street, not wanting any trouble.

'Where is everybody?' thought Bob. 'Flippin' typical!' He sat down by one of those waterfalls that have plastic palm trees and things dripping round the edge. Brenton was what they called a 'new town'. What that meant was that they had found a bit of space outside London near the country, and had built a town on it. Everything about it was plastic ... palm trees, neon lights, hamburgers, people and credit cards. It was probably a nice idea at the time the planners put it down on paper, but in practice, well ... it's hard for East London's overspill to adapt itself to that kind of living.

12

There was surprisingly little graffiti, but on the other hand it wasn't the kind of material that you could easily write on. "Another fun-packed night on the town in good old Brenton. Whoopee!" sighed Bob.

'Well,' he thought, 'I can see that all this excitement is going to be too much for me. I might as well push off home.' Bob had been sitting on the same bench for half an hour; if he was honest he would have to admit that there wasn't a lot to choose from tonight. He either sat on this hard wooden bench, freezing to death, or he went home. If he went home his dad would ask him where he'd been and he would have to say nowhere and then his dad would think he was being cheeky and they would start their usual row. Bob put his fists up to his chin and leant his elbows on his knees. 'There is nothing, NOTHING, absolutely nothing going for me! This town should be declared a disaster area. There's not a soul about, the fag machine don't work, and I can't remember the last time I saw a decent looking bird hanging around.'

Just then three rather large blokes seemed to appear from nowhere. 'Hallo,' thought Bob, 'what have we here? I don't remember seeing them around before.' As if by magic, a little kid popped out from behind one of them and shouted, "That's him! He's the one! He beat me up when we were breaking! He's the one!"

Bob got up.

"Just a minute, mate," sneered the largest of the three. "I think we might want a word with you. What do you think your game is, eh? Pushing over little kids? Spoiling all their fun?"

Bob swallowed hard and then put on a false grin. "Hang on, mate, you've got it all wrong! We were just having a laugh, the kid'll tell you! It was just a bit of a joke."

"That's strange," said another one, "I don't see anyone laughing, do you, Alan? Brian? No, nor me."

"I hear you're pretty good at breakdancing," grinned Brian. "Well, come on, don't be shy! We wanna see, don't we lads?"

Now Bob wasn't a coward by any means, but these were three hefty blokes, probably around eighteen or nineteen years old, and Bob was nearly sixteen. He was totally outclassed and outnumbered.

"Give it a rest, mate. Anyway, there's no music," said Bob, pointing to their empty hands.

"Oh, so you want some rhythm, eh? The stinking lad who beat up my brother wants a beat of his own." And with that the three of them began a slow handclap, and then they started chanting, "Dance! Dance! Dance!" There was no way out. Bob started to dance and as he put his hands on the floor, they started to kick his hands away, just as he had kicked Brian's little brother ... only they didn't stop. To Bob it seemed to go on and on. He remembered yelling and then heard one of them say, "Quick! Someone's coming," and just as they had appeared, they disappeared down the other side of the town.

Bob started to get up. His head hurt, his ribs hurt and his body felt as if it were on fire. Suddenly he heard footsteps running towards him — "No!" he shouted. Then he looked up and saw Terry Ellis staring down at him. He knew Terry vaguely, they went to the same school but right now he couldn't even remember his *own* name, let alone Terry's.

"All right, mate, take it easy. Cor, you're in a mess.

No, don't try to get up, stay there a minute." Bob felt Terry's jacket cover his shoulders. Bob wanted to lie there for ever, he'd never been beaten up three against one ... well, not that way round, anyway. He gradually felt a bit better so Terry helped him to the bench. Bob groaned and leaned against the back of the bench. "Thanks, mate."

Terry went over to the fountain, brought back some water in a discarded paper cup and started to mop Bob's face. "Ow! That stings!" cried Bob.

"I should think that's the least of your problems. What happened?" asked Terry. Bob lowered his eyes and said, "Well, you know how it is, some guys think they're tough when they're in a crowd."

"You don't sound very certain," remarked Terry, trying to wring his blood-soaked handkerchief out. Bob just grunted in reply.

Terry looked at Bob. He knew him, of course. He was known at school as 'Bob the Yob' and from what Terry had seen, they were not far wrong. Still, Bob came from a rough end of town and Terry had heard that his dad was a bit of a villain himself, so perhaps it wasn't all Bob's fault. 'It's so easy to point the finger,' thought Terry, 'just because of looks or what side of town you live on, people judge you. If you're well-off you're all right but if you're poor, then you must be a hard-nut.' He wasn't the type of boy to easily dismiss someone, but at the same time he was wary of them.

Deciding to take Bob at his word, he said, "These blokes, did you know them at all?"

"Never seen 'em before ... Ow!" cried Bob.

"Sorry." Terry tried again, "So how come they beat you up, what did they say?"

"Cor, you're worse than my old man, all these questions! Look, I was beaten up, all right? I was walking around minding my own business and these fellas decided to have some fun and I was the only bloke around. Satisfied?" As he spoke, Bob could have bitten his tongue off. After all, Terry was only trying to help, and now he looked quite hurt. 'Yeh, well, I'm not used to people tending my wounds, am I?' thought Bob. "Anyway, what brings you into town? I've never seen you hanging round, you always strike me as the kind of bloke who goes round someone's house of a night. Y'know, playing records an' that," said Bob.

Terry laughed. "Hit it right on the head, Bob! I'm on my way over to Martin Heyward's, do you know him? Brown hair, glasses?"

Bob nodded and tried not to remember the times he had menaced Martin, or that other time when he had nicked his football jersey from him. "Yeh," he said, "I know him."

"You can come over if you like, Martin wouldn't mind. His parents have gone out and they let him use this brilliant stereo system!" he explained. He was trying to imagine Bob sitting in Martin's front room ... all that plush off-white carpet and Bob's Doc Martins.

"No, I don't think so, I'm not really in the right mood for company, I think I'd better go home," replied Bob.

"You sure you're all right? I've got to go that way, so I'll walk down to the end with you," offered Terry.

As they walked, they chatted a bit politely, the way you do when you don't really know someone well and you're not sure what to say to please them. "Cold tonight, I knew I should have brought a coat instead of this jacket ..." As Terry spoke they both looked down at his jacket. It had smears of blood down the front and it looked as if it had been draped across a muddy pavement — which it had.

Bob felt quite ashamed (a totally new experience for him) and said, "Sorry about your jacket, Tell."

Terry could have kicked himself, what a stupid comment to make! "Oh, that's all right, it's an old one," he lied (a totally new experience for *him*!). "I normally use it for school."

"You run that whatsit club, don't you?" remarked Bob.

"The Christian Union," said Terry.

"Yeh, that's it," Bob said. "Do you really believe in all that then?" he asked.

"That's a pretty broad question, but if you mean am I a Christian, then the answer is ... yes," replied Terry. "From the look on your face I gather the thought doesn't appeal too much to you then?"

"I've never really thought about it. I suppose I'm not the type to get involved in that sort of thing, it's more for people like you isn't it?"

"People like me? What's *that* supposed to mean?" Terry looked slightly annoyed.

"Well, I mean ... " Bob struggled for the right words, he didn't want to insult this bloke who had just saved his bacon. "Well ... it's for a better type of person." He laughed to himself, "God's hardly likely to want me for a sunbeam, is he?" To his surprise, Terry laughed back. He wasn't sure whether he laughed to be polite, or whether it was the thought of Bob the Yob dressed up as a sunbeam. "You could do a lot worse you know," said Terry. "You never know when you're going to

17

need a friend, and that's what God could be to you."

"Yeh, well talking of friends, thanks for your help but I'd better be off now. See you, OK?" With that, Bob started off down the road. Terry stood there watching him go with a sinking sort of feeling. 'I wonder if I carved that up? Lord, it was him that brought the subject up, asking me if I believed in you. I hope I haven't put him off.' He turned round and looked once more back up the arcade, the electric clock on the wall said it was 21.35 and that there were 'more bargains at Woolies than anywhere else'.

'Oh no, half past nine!' thought Terry. 'I'd better get round to Martin's before it's time to come back!'

Martin's parents owned a large detached house in Sandwell Road. They lived in Brenton, but only just, and referred to the area as Sandwell. Mr. and Mrs. Heyward were nice people, you know the sort ... nice house, nice cat, nice furniture, nice garden — nice, nice, nice! Martin, however, was dead ordinary. He was just how Terry had described him — brown hair and glasses. He was totally unaffected by the middle-class attitude of his parents, as far as he was concerned a jogging suit was a jogging suit whether it came from the market or whether it had Nike or something written on it. A mug was something you drank tea out of, whether it was plastic or Wedgewood, and normally he would have absolutely no idea about fashion and certainly didn't care about clothes. Apart from now, this moment, as he opened the door to Terry.

"Good grief, Terry! Your jacket!" cried Martin. "What on *earth* happened! Your mum only bought you that last week, she'll go up the wall!" As usual when Martin got excited about anything, his glasses careered from one side of his nose to the other despite all efforts to keep them on straight. He had the look of an absent-minded professor. All he needed was a microscope and a test tube!

"Hang on, calm down," said Terry. "It's not as bad as it looks." Let's face it, it looked awful.

"Blood!" yelled Martin. "Blood! What happened? Were you knocked down? Quick, come inside, I'll phone for an ambulance!" The glasses were well away by this time, the arms were flailing about and the brown wavy hair was doing its own version of morris dancing.

Terry joined in the arm waving, only he was trying to get Martin to quieten down enough to tell him that it wasn't *his* blood.

"Martin! Martin! Hello, are you receiving me? I am *not* hurt, I repeat, I am *not* hurt!" Terry's hands were cupped round his mouth as he exaggerated his message. By now, he had managed to move into the front room, throw his jacket on the chair and sit on it.

"Now," he said. "If you're ready, I'll tell you what happened. For a kick-off, the blood doesn't belong to me, it belongs to Bobby Harris."

Martin interrupted immediately. "Bobby Harris! You had a fight with Bob Harris?" Then he paused, working the situation out. "No, hang on, if you'd had a fight with him, he'd have flattened you."

"Thanks for the vote of confidence! Anyway, you're right, I didn't fight him ..." and Terry proceeded to tell his friend what had happened.

"So you believed him then?" asked Martin.

"I think that whether I believed his story or not is ir-relevant. What I'm concerned about is that I think we may have misjudged him a bit. He got quite serious for a minute when he asked me if I believed in God." Terry looked thoughtful. "After all, what do we know about him really?"

"Well, I can tell you what I know." Martin got up and walked over to the record player. "I know he nicked my best football jersey ... and he's walloped me once, as well."

Strains of Dire Straits wafted from the beautiful stereo (his mum and dad didn't actually like music, but they thought it added a touch of class to the room). "Well, I think we should give him a chance," stated Terry.

"How do you mean?"

"One of the purposes of me coming round here tonight was to discuss the Christian Union, right? And the main problem, as we all know, is how to get people interested. So far, we've just asked our friends to come — but what about people like Bob? I mean, he's shown more interest tonight than most of my friends have shown all term! So perhaps we've been barking up the wrong tree!"

Martin reeled back a bit. "Terry, you aren't seriously suggesting that we ask Bob and people like him to *our* Christian Union ... are you?"

"Yes, Martin, I am," said Terry.

"Somehow," ventured Martin, "I don't think that the Christian Union is going to be a hundred per cent behind this idea."

Terry pursed his lips. "What about you?"

. . . . .

Bob was nearly home. It had taken longer than usual because his ribs still ached and his legs didn't feel like they really belonged to him. Bob had had time to think as he went home, and he was trying to sort out in his mind what he thought about Terry and that brief conversation they had had. He admitted to himself that he had been grateful for Terry's help, but what was it about him that made you talk about yourself? Bob had never really confided in anybody, and yet he had found himself asking Terry Ellis about God! Strange.

He heard someone laugh and looked up to see a couple of girls coming towards him. 'Oh great!' he thought. 'Here am I looking the biggest state the world has ever seen, and down the road comes that girl from our school! It's too late to cross over.' Bob had liked her for quite a while now. She was in the fourth year, had blond shiny hair, always seemed to be laughing and rushing around everywhere. 'Much too popular to notice me anyway,' thought Bob. 'Still, maybe one day ...'

They walked past. Bob looked straight ahead of him.

"Cor, what a state," the dark one said.

"Think he's been drinking? Wonder what he looks like when he's sober," giggled the blonde one.

"Honestly, Carol Ellis, you are a laugh!" At this they joined arms and giggled again, as they made their way home.

Bob looked back. Had he heard right??

2

The Summons

"Is that the first bell or the second bell?" A curious looking individual asked his mate.

"I think it's the first," replied Pete. "Eh, watch it, mate!" School was full of kids who thought that the quickest way to get anywhere was to walk through everyone else.

Brenton Comp. was very much in keeping with Brenton shopping arcade. It was incredibly modern and looked more like an airport than a school. There were spaces just like airport waiting rooms for school-kids to hang around in instead of playgrounds, and this loudspeaker system that announced notices instead of landing times. Just as Simon and Pete walked past one, it hooted at them.

"Cor, right in my ear! Why can't we have notices slipped in the register like everyone else?" complained Pete.

"Attention please, will Bob Harris please report to the headmaster's room. Bob Harris to headmaster's room. Thank you." You never knew whose voice was going to come out of the speaker. Usually it was the school secretary who fancied herself as a train station

22

announcer. She had this piercing squawk that would have done a parrot proud, and if you happened to be standing next to the system when it came on — it nearly blew your head off. Other times it was the head, who obviously didn't like using a microphone. You could tell by the way he always blew on it and tapped the top before his immortal words "Are you sure it's on?" came flowing out and down the corridors. Today the announcement came via the screeching secretary.

"Sounds like Bob's in trouble again." This comment came from Pete and it was more of a statement than a sneer. Pete was not the kind of boy to judge people unless he knew them well and he had never really met Bob. (Most people would say that *that* was one of life's little advantages.)

"I wonder what he's done?" said Simon. He had a great fear of being called over the system, even if it was for something good! He worried about what other people thought. He was forever asking other people's opinions on subjects ... "Do you think one page is enough for tonight's maths homework?" ... "Are you taking art or music as an extra?" ... "Is that the first or the second bell?"

Why he worried so much no one knew. It could have been because he was fat and thought that people were judging him all the time, but then again, he wasn't *that* fat, he was just rotund. It ran (or rolled) in his family so he was quite happy at home, surrounded by other happily round people. But for some reason, he needed to be liked and therefore worried about his reputation. Having said that, he was just as likely to ignore your advice once given and do the total opposite!

"Brrrrrrrrrriiiiiiiiinnnnggggg!" The second bell

went.

Second bell always caused an incredible amount of havoc when it went. It seemed that everyone at one end of the school needed to be at the other end and vice versa. To see it in action was rather like watching a rugby scrum with 500 kids on each side. The noise was tremendous — a thousand kids all screaming "see you at break" etc., and being carried along on a tide of brief cases, satchels, ties, crisp packets and plastic lunch boxes.

School had officially begun for the day.

In room B5 Carol was sitting at her desk with the lid up reading the latest copy of Smash Hits and sighing over a photo of Duran Duran. What would she do if when she left school at the end of the day, there was a flashy car stopping near where she was walking, and then one of the dark coloured windows rolled down and Simon Le Bon put his head out of the window and said, "Excuse me, can you tell me where the Odeon is?" She would smile her best smile and say, "Well, it's quite difficult to explain ..." and then he would say, "Look, I wonder if you would mind having a lift and showing us (us??) where this place is?" And as she got in, their eyes would meet and ... "Carol Ellis!!" Mr. Wood yelled. "If I have to ask you one more time, I am going to come over there and slam that desk lid on your empty head! Now put it down and join in with the rest of us. Thank you." The 'thank you' was delivered with just the right amount of sarcasm by Mr. Wood who was in fact a very good teacher. Carol normally paid more attention in his lessons than most, but when you are a fourteen year old girl, there is *so* much more to think about than just English lessons. Now where was she?

Oh yes, Simon Le Bon had just looked into her eyes and they had realised straight away that there could never be anyone else for either of them ...

Carol's friend Sharon looked over and whispered to her, "Hey! What's so important?"

Carol gave her lazy smile. "Oh, nothing much. I was just day dreaming."

Her friend gave her a wise knowing sort of look, "Oh yes, what's his name?"

"Simon Le Bon if you *must* know!" laughed Carol and for a change opened the book on her desk to the right page.

"What are you doing lunch time?" Sharon asked.

"Same as usual, I suppose. Go to the loo, put some make-up on, do my hair, catch up on the latest gossip ..." Carol replied.

"Here, talking of gossip, you remember that bloke we saw last night when we were coming home? You know, we thought he was drunk and that?" asked Sharon.

"Last night? Oh yeh, I know, scruffy bloke with blond hair. Yeh, what about him? Don't tell me — he's asked you out!!" Carol giggled behind her English book.

Sharon blushed furiously. "No, nothing like that! No, it was him that got called up in front of Mr. Lemming this morning! I wonder what he's done?"

"Who cares?" Carol started to look bored with the conversation since it had no romantic entanglements any more.

Carol Ellis was very much a typical teenage girl. Constantly looking at herself in the mirror, terrified of spots and split ends, always fancying someone and then running a mile if they spoke to her. When you are fourteen you are neither a child nor an adult, so sometimes you need someone to help you and sometimes you can manage quite well by yourself thank you very much. It was probably for this reason that Carol looked up to her older brother Terry. She always found she could talk to him and he didn't laugh at her. She knew that lots of her friends found Terry attractive and so secretly she was very proud of him. The only thing that drove her mad was that he *would* flaunt his Christianity! She didn't mind him being a Christian, and anyway she went to church with him herself most Sundays, there was nothing wrong with that — but did he have to make the whole thing so public?

As if hearing her thoughts the sound system came on with its awful hoot. "Attention, please! The Christian Union will be meeting this lunchtime in room C6. Those interested please be there at 12.45." The parrot squawked on about the fact that since it was raining, the gym would be used for lunchtime training for the school football team and that if you had to go to the meeting for the visit to Switzerland next year, would you please get an early lunch as you would need to be in B3 by 12.30.

As the Christian Union meeting was mentioned, everyone turned round and looked at Carol. Terry ran the C.U. and the fact that she was his sister somehow gave everyone licence to stare at her every time it was mentioned.

"Perhaps Carol could read page fifty-three to us?" Good old Mr. Wood! There were times when he could come to the rescue like that and steer everybody's attention away from one thing and on to another.

"Thanks, sir!" said Carol under her breath, and proceeded to read the page with great precision ... even though she hadn't a clue what it was about.

"Now, Carol, in a few words, what do you think the author was trying to put over in this scene?" Mr. Wood waited patiently.

"Well," said Carol, stalling for time.

BBBBBRRRRRIIIIINNNNGGGGG!!

"Saved by the bell!" cried Carol amidst the confusion of shutting desk lids, screeching of chairs and general din. She started to pack her bag. There was that lovely picture of Simon again! Sigh!

"Carol!" It was Sharon. "Carol! Come on, I'm not going to stand here all day!"

"OK, Sharon!" shouted Carol as she left the room.

. . . . .

At 12.45 ten people walked dutifully into room C6. Terry was already there, sat at the front of the classroom waiting for the rest of the Christian Union members to appear. Tuesday was not their usual day for C.U. so Terry was only expecting the dedicated ones to arrive.

Martin came in just before the rest. He had just finished an interesting session in the metalwork room. You could tell by the way the iron filings clung to his jumper.

Pete came through the door next, with Simon bringing up the rear ... "Yes, but what would *you* have done, Pete? I thought mine was a pretty good answer but now I'm not so sure...."

"Don't worry about it, Simon, it's not that important," groaned Pete and quickly found a seat by the radiator and collapsed onto it.

The other six vaguely arrived together, as if they had all been standing outside plucking up the courage to go

27

in (which they had). Safety in numbers an' all that! It took at least ten minutes for this little crowd to get themselves sorted out and sat down. Helen and Avril wanted to sit where they always sat, but two of the others got there before them so they had to be content to sit somewhere else. Both of these girls were Christians and they both had parents who were 'something in the church' so it followed in their logic that they should have the best seats! Having sorted out this problem, Terry went to call the meeting to something vaguely resembling order. Simon immediately got out his sandwiches. "Simon, I wonder if they could possibly wait until a little later, I really would like your attention." Terry smiled patiently as he said this. It wasn't Simon's fault really.

"Right! I'm sorry to call you here on a Tuesday, but I thought it was important to ..." began Terry.

"Aren't we going to have any singing to start with?" Avril's mouth asked this question, although it always seemed to come from her nose. "We usually have a chorus or something," she grumbled.

"No, Avril. This isn't the normal meeting, so we're not doing the normal thing. OK?" replied Terry (he had a speech prepared and he was gradually losing it ...) "Martin and I were having a discussion the other evening and there are a few things we would like to put to you." Martin started to look uncomfortable; all of a sudden he had taken a great interest in his shoes.

"So far, we have only really invited our close friends to these meetings, and something happened the other evening to make me feel that perhaps we should branch out more," said Terry.

Nine heads looked up in surprise. What could he mean? This is *our* meeting! We like it like this! It wouldn't be the same with other people!

"Can you explain what you mean by branching out?" asked Helen.

"I'm coming to that, but first I'd like to tell you about an incident that happened to me the other evening, and then perhaps you'll understand my statement."

Terry went through how he walked into town and met Bob. He glossed over the fight and concentrated on telling them how Bob had made tentative enquiries about the Christian Union and in fact about whether God could care for someone like him.

"He didn't say a lot, but I was just surprised that he had even thought about it. And then it struck me that there might be a lot of people like Bob in the school who have seen notices about the C.U. but don't really know what goes on here," explained Terry.

"I mean," put in Martin, "they have as much right to know that God cares for them as anyone else." Everyone turned and stared at Martin who went red and wished he hadn't said anything. He went back to looking at his shoes.

"Well ..." said Terry. "Let's have some reaction!"

There was a stony silence for a few minutes, then some of them started shifting around in the chairs. Avril blew her nose and Simon went for his sandwiches.

"Oh come on! You must have something to say!" Terry was looking exasperated.

"You really think we should ask the likes of Bob Harris to our Christian Union meetings?" asked Pete.

Terry nodded.

"OK, so how do we go about doing that? I mean, I don't think it will be as easy as saying, 'Hello, Bob, why don't you come along to the C.U. on Wednesday'!" retorted Pete.

"Anybody else?" asked Terry.

"I don't know any rough kids, so I can't ask them," said Helen flatly.

"If you don't mind me saying," put in Simon, "I think we had better sort our own priorities out. What's a Christian Union for?"

"Simon's right," said Terry. "We have to decide whether the Christian Union is for Christians only, or whether it's for getting other people interested as well."

A voice at the back said, "Most after-school clubs are for those that are interested in whatever the subject is. They're all looking for supporters."

"Yes, well there's no point in joining the squash club unless you can play squash!" snapped back Avril.

Terry waved his arms in the air. "OK, how many people think it's a good idea to invite non-Christians to the C.U.?"

Six hands and a sandwich went up in the air.

"Well that's a majority. Right! Any ideas for inviting people along?"

"Hang on!" said Pete. "I think we should talk about exactly *why* they are being invited first!"

"The priority," began Terry, "of any Christian, is to tell other people about Jesus. We have all found Jesus to be the most wonderful thing in our lives and it should be natural to share Him with everyone else. However, I think we have to be careful, we don't want people thinking we are just out scalp-hunting, if you see what I mean. So let's have some ideas."

"How about a film or a video?" suggested one. "We could get 'The Cross and the Switchblade' or something and advertise it over the sound system!"

"Good!" Terry was feeling encouraged. "Anyone else?"

"How about a debate?" cried Martin. "We could think up a subject like 'Is God the cause of War?' and put up a good fight for Christianity! We would need to get someone in from outside school, though. Someone with a bit of knowledge about the subject who could give everyone the facts and that. Maybe a Christian soldier or something!" Martin was well away now. Debates were right up his street.

"That could turn into a war in the classroom if we didn't handle it right," put in Helen.

"OK, so we have to handle it right ... we can do that!" said Martin.

"How about 'Is God for real?' — I mean, that's what most people want to know, isn't it?" asked Pete.

"Yeh, but it's not such an exciting theme as war, is it?" asked Martin.

"Well, it seems like we are all in favour, anyway," commented Terry. This wasn't going entirely according to his schedule, but at least it had got everybody animated. He always felt a bit ashamed of Helen and Avril. It wasn't that they were not good Christians, because in their own way, they were. It was just that they had this high and mighty attitude, and he knew for a fact that this was the sole reason his sister Carol didn't go to the C.U.

Carol had quite a hard time with church and things like that. She could see nothing wrong in believing in God, it was jus. l these other things they made you do ... like going to church and C.U. meetings where she always felt as if she were the outsider, the one who everybody looked down on. Somehow it was as if they couldn't accept her as a Christian.

Carol was so opposite to Helen and Avril, that it was quite impossible to put them in the same room. Yet Carol always felt that Christians should be able to cope with each other's personalities. At this moment, Terry felt exactly the same. 'How am I supposed to cope with all these people and bring in new ones to the meeting?' He brushed his fingers through his well-groomed hair. 'Well, Lord, this one's up to you.' Aloud he said, "Right! It's nearly time to go, so let's meet back here on Wednesday and discuss our plan of action."

There was a mad scramble as he finished speaking. 'Now I know how our teachers feel,' he thought to himself ....

Earlier on that day, Bob had heard his name announced on the sound system. He was with a couple of his mates at the time and they immediately poked him in the ribs and clumped him on the back. "Go to it, Bob. Tell him what you think," and other such phrases that were supposed to make Bob feel better. As it happened, he wasn't feeling all that brilliant. Having been beaten up the night before he'd had enough. He had gone home and was hoping to sneak upstairs before his dad saw him, but his luck was well and truly out.

"That you, Bob?" grunted a voice that sounded like it had been drowning in cheap wine.

"Yeh," he answered. "I'm going upstairs, I've got a lot of homework, be down later, all right?"

"No, it's not all right. I've been sitting here for hours waiting for you to get home. I ain't had no tea or nothing. You'd best get yourself in that kitchen and get your poor old dad something to eat and drink," he moaned.

"Sounds to me like you've had plenty to drink," muttered Bob under his breath.

"What was that?" yelled Dad.

"Do you want beans on toast or what?" yelled back Bob who had grudgingly made his way to the kitchen. There was no answer from Mr. Harris but that was not uncommon, so Bob just carried on throwing bread under the grill and opening a tin of beans. While the toast burnt, Bob began thinking of the night's events and the way that Terry Ellis had turned up just in the nick of time. 'Not a bad bloke really,' thought Bob. But what was really on his mind was the fact that he could have sworn he heard that brunette call that blond Carol Ellis as he had been limping home. He knew her name was Carol, but he hadn't managed to find out her second name. 'So what? Ellis is a dead common name. She's probably no relation at all ... but on the other hand ....'

"What you doin' to that toast, it smells like the Black Hole of Calcutta from here!" Bob's dad was good at moaning, it was what he excelled in.

"All right, all right, keep your hair on!" shouted Bob. Why was beans on toast one of the most frustrating things to cook? Everything cooks at once, the toast, the beans and if you've got a kettle on as well, you're done for.

Putting all these things on a tray, Bob braced himself and entered the front room with a smile on his face. "Here we are, Pop! Just the way you like it."

"What on earth is THAT!" His dad looked furious.

"It's beans on toast. Look, I'm sorry mate, but if you want something else, you'll have to do it yourself."

"I'm not talking about the food, I'm talking about that on your face," yelled his dad. "What have you been doing?"

Bob put his hand up to his face and felt an enormous

swelling. He stepped over to the mirror ... looking back at him was this bloke with what amounted to half a face. A gigantic black eye, a cut on the other cheek, and grazes all over the place.

"I ..." began Bob.

"If you're going to tell me that you've been mugged, you can save your breath. Just what are you trying to do to yourself? Why can't you behave yourself for a change like ... like ..."

"You?" yelled back Bob and calmly walked out of the door.

What was the use? There was no point in trying to explain what had happened, he might as well not bother.

... so now, here he was, sat outside the headmaster's room waiting to be summoned. Mr. Lemming wasn't too bad, actually, as far as headmasters went, but he was still a headmaster, and he had still called Bob Harris to his office. Bob didn't mind being told off, but he hated having to wait outside — as if it wasn't bad enough being announced on the system, you had to stand here as a constant reminder to everyone.

"Harris!" Mr. Lemming's glasses appeared round the corner of the door.

"Come in, will you." You almost expected him to add "there's a good chap" but he never did. Once inside, it was a whole new ball game. You were never asked to sit down or anything, you just had to stand there feeling a right wally, and wait until he spoke to you. Sometimes he would shuffle about with files and books, and you could swear it was all done on purpose, to make you feel more nervous.

34

3

Whose Side Are You On?

"How's your father?" enquired the head. "Still no job?"

'Ah ha!' thought Bob, 'it's the subtle ploy!'

"He's all right, I suppose," answered Bob. "You're right about the work, by the way." Bob considered Mr. Lemming. Was he buttering him up for something? Perhaps he had bad news! 'Nah, I'm just going to get a rollicking for something or other. I wish he'd stop playing games.'

"I hear you've found a new friend. I must say I'm surprised. I didn't think you were the sort that would hang around together," remarked the head.

"A new ...? Do what?" replied Bob.

"It's been brought to my notice ..." ('Here it comes,' thought Bob) "that you and young Terry Ellis were up to no good the other night. Some sort of fight in the precinct in town ... am I right?"

"No!" said Bob emphatically. "Well, yes but no." (Good grief this was an awkward one.)

"Well, come on, boy, either you were there, or someone's just seen your double. I haven't much time to spare this morning, so it would save me a lot of time if you could tell me exactly what you and Ellis were up to."

"We weren't up to nothing!" Bob was so used to saying this, that it felt quite weird to be saying it and not lying.

"I sometimes wonder why we bother to teach you the English language, Harris," sighed Mr. Lemming. "Now come along, just tell me what happened and then we can sort this out. I have it on the good authority of Mr. Bellamy that you were involved in a fight and by the look of you I think we can assume that this is correct."

'Oh great, Bellamy!' thought Bob. 'Now it all makes sense.'

Mr. Bellamy was the deputy headmaster and he was totally detestable. This wasn't just Bob's opinion, most of the kids found him intolerable. He was sneaky and shifty and very obviously after the headmaster's job, so if ever anything went slightly wrong, he was down on you like a ton of bricks. If you came to school late, say, missed assembly, any other teacher would tell you off and forget it. Not so Bellamy. He would make a complete idiot out of you the next day, making you stand for assembly while everybody else sat down — that kind of thing. He wasn't very well liked by most of the staff either, but because he carried the title 'Deputy' you had to be careful.

"… and saw you and Ellis walking away from the precinct. You covered in blood and Ellis with his sleeves rolled up," the headmaster blabbed on and on. "So, what have you got to say for yourself?" He had that 'I'm waiting' look on his face.

"OK, I'll admit I was in a fight. But it wasn't my

fault, I was set on by a gang of blokes all older than me. And Terry Ellis just happened to come along and so they ran off," explained Bob.

"They saw Terry Ellis coming so they all ran off," quoted the headmaster. "Do you take me for a complete idiot, Harris?" he yelled. "Terry Ellis is hardly the kind of boy who is going to make a gang of older boys run off!"

"No, what I meant was that they heard him coming round the corner, so they took off before they saw who it was." Telling the truth was hard, it always seemed to land you in more trouble than fabricating a little bit. 'I bet if I'd said I'd been run over by a runaway Sainsbury trolley, he'd have believed me,' thought Bob.

"Well, Harris, as you seem to be unable to even put a decent explanation to Mr. Bellamy's witness, I think we will have both you and Ellis in detention." Mr. Lemming closed his book, signifying that the case for the prosecution was closed.

"But, Mr. Lemming, that's not fair!" Bob leaned over the head's desk (a very silly thing to do).

"Are you threatening me, boy?" Mr. Lemming looked angry now. He had already missed the first five minutes of the radio programme he listened to every day.

"No, of course not, but you don't understand ..." said Bob.

"I understand," replied the head. "Out!"

Bob turned and stalked out — this was one door he couldn't slam, but he would have loved to have done.

. . . . .

"Here, Carol! If Miss Mitchell catches you with that nail varnish on, she'll go barmy," gasped Sharon.

Carol smiled and looked at her nails, then holding her hands at arms length she admired them again. "Yeh, but they're nice, aren't they? Perhaps I should lend her the bottle, what do you think?"

The girls went into gales of laughter at the thought of the fifty year old spinster wearing purple nail varnish.

Sharon leant on the nearest sink (the girls' loo was the only place to go for a break from school life). "What do you think I should do with my hair, Carol? I wish I had hair like yours." In fact, half the girls in the school wished they had hair like Carol, it was so blond and natural and just casually waved where it wanted to.

"Why don't you go blond?" asked Carol, looking at Sharon's mousey hair.

"Blond? Me? You've got to be joking! Anyway, if Miss Mitchell doesn't like nail varnish, I can't see her going for dyed blondes in a big way either," Sharon said.

"Terry likes blond hair," said Carol casually, and watched as Sharon reacted.

"Knowing your brother, he would only like natural blondes anyway and mine would have roots as black as anything growing out of it within a fortnight," laughed Sharon.

"But you'd do it if you thought it would improve your chances, would you?" asked Carol, with visions of Terry and her best friend together.

"Improve my chances? What are you on about?" Sharon was looking away from Carol, but could see her quite clearly in the mirror. Somehow it wasn't as bad as looking straight at her when talking about Terry.

"You and Terry. Oh come on, Sharon, I know you fancy him." Carol was provoking Sharon something

38

awful, but she was dying to know if she did actually care about her brother.

"I thought he was going out with Tracey What's-her-name," said Sharon.

"Tracey? No way. She thinks she's in with a chance and she tells people she's going out with him, but she's not. I mean, I should know, I am his sister!" Once again Carol's eyes took on the proud look she reserved for Terry. "So come on, how are we going to get you together with Terry?"

"Now, Carol, this has gone far enough, you can't make people fancy each other, you know. It doesn't work like that," scolded Sharon.

Carol turned round with a meaningful look. "Oh doesn't it?" she said. "We'll see," and with that, she left.

· · · · ·

Mr. Bellamy strolled down the corridor as only he could. Hands behind his back, sergeant major air about him. He hadn't actually made it to sergeant in the army and had always seen it as a personal insult. "You, boy! Take that coat off, it should be in the cloakroom! You there, where do you think you're going? Have you got permission? Wilkins! Report to me after break ..." and so it went on. Mr. Bellamy was a bit like one of those Action Men, you pull a string at the back of him and all these sayings start spewing out. Today he was on the lookout for Terry Ellis. It would give him a great deal of satisfaction to speak to the boy personally before his name was called on the sound system. As far as Bellamy was concerned, Ellis was much too nice, and it annoyed him. As if hearing his thoughts, Terry came running

39

round the corner.

"Ellis!"

Terry heard his name and stopped in mid-stride. "Oh no, Bellamy! Trust me to be running in a walk-zone!' "Sorry, sir," said Terry.

"In a hurry are we, Ellis? Perhaps you were hoping I wouldn't see you. But then, that's what you must have been hoping last night as well, eh boy?" Bellamy looked at him expectantly.

"Sorry, sir?" Terry didn't like this teacher any more than his mates but he didn't normally get stopped by him.

"It's not worth playing the innocent with me, son. I know most people only know you as the C.U. leader. But we know better, don't we? Eh? Eh?"

Terry looked puzzled.

Bellamy pointed up to one of the sound system speakers.

"Any minute now, that system will go and do you know what it will be for?" asked Mr. B.

"No, sir," answered Terry. Really, what was he on about?

"It will be the headmaster summoning you to his office. Yes, you may well look shocked. But I'm afraid your luck ran out this time, lad, because I saw you in that fight last night. You and Bob Harris ...." As he went to finish his pompous speech, the system came on and sure enough after much blowing down the mike, Mr. Lemming's voice was heard to say, "Will Terry Ellis please report to my room. Terry Ellis. Thank you."

Terry just couldn't believe he was hearing right! In the first place, there was no way that Mr. Bellamy could have seen Terry fighting, simply because he hadn't been. In the second place, why hadn't Terry seen Mr. Bellamy?

Terry knocked rather too hurriedly on the headmaster's door. He was feeling such a mixture of righteous anger and confusion, that he had not really thought about what he should say to the head.

"Come."

Terry walked into the room. The head looked up almost immediately (pretty unusual for him) and said, "Ah, yes."

Terry didn't say a word, he just stood there waiting for the onslaught.

"Well, Ellis, I must say I am disappointed in you. Disappointed that someone of your character should stoop so low as to cause a fight in a public place. Mr. Bellamy tells me he was sitting in McDonald's when he glanced across and saw you and this Harris boy, fighting like a couple of punks. Now, I won't have it!" he said sternly.

"Sir! That's not the truth! I was helping Bob who had been beaten up by some other fellows!" Terry cried.

"Hmm, so you have conspired to tell the same story. It's worse than I thought. I might have expected Bob Harris to come up with something like this, but as he tells me you were both in it together, I see no alternative," the head looked serious.

"Sir!" How could Terry call the deputy head a liar?

"Detention. Wednesday night, both of you. See Mr. Bellamy before you leave. That's all." Mr. Lemming waved his hand towards the door, which obviously meant it was time for Terry to leave.

Terry was stunned. It wasn't that he had never had

41

detention before, because he had, but that was more for mucking about than anything. However, he had never been in this sort of trouble.

'I shall have to find Bob,' thought Terry.

As it happened, Bob was also trying to find Terry, but in a school of a thousand pupils, that's not always easy ....

So it wasn't until Wednesday that they met again. Terry was on his way to his C.U. meeting and he was already late. He was trying to think of how he was going to explain to the rest of the members about tonight's detention.

Bob was rushing around trying to think how to explain to Terry about the same thing!

"Oi!" yelled Bob.

Terry looked round and saw Bob Harris coming towards him. He felt a bit awkward and so he gulped and said, "Hi, how's your face now?"

"All right, I suppose," said Bob. "Listen, about this detention ...."

"Don't worry, I'll see you after school in the detention room and we can discuss it then, OK?" Terry tried to look cheerful and then ran off in the opposite direction in search of his C.U. members.

Terry dashed into C6 and as he entered, everything went quiet. "Sorry I'm late." Terry looked round the room and everyone sat there and looked back at him.

There was a sort of cough from the front row and Pete nudged Martin who got to his feet and said, "Before we start this meeting, there's something that I, er ... we would like to know. Em ... apparently there is a rumour going round that you and Bob Harris ..."

Terry nearly exploded.

42

"Oh yes, thank you very much, that's exactly what I need. My own Christian Union members to give me the once-over! I thought at least I could trust you to realise there's been a mistake."

The front row fidgeted. "Oh no, we were just wondering really ..." started Pete.

"What he's trying to say," put in Helen, "is that, if this is what happens by just being sociable to people like Bob Harris, what is the point in trying to bring them in to something like the Christian Union?" There were a few mumbles of "yes, right, exactly".

"The point," said Terry, trying very very hard to keep his patience, "is that if more people put their trust in Jesus to help them through their rough times ... there wouldn't be people like Bob carving their lives up all the time! How can I get it through to you that being a Christian isn't like joining the Guides or Scouts ... it's not an exclusive club, it's for everyone. Everyone in this school needs Jesus.

Again there was a silence. Then a voice spoke up. It was Simon.

"You know, Terry's right. Jesus didn't care if His reputation got torn to ribbons. He was seen with just about every outcast in town."

"And if Jesus can care for those sort of people, then so can we ... or at least we should give it a try ..." put in someone else.

Terry stood up. "Look, folks, I know this week hasn't been very normal so far, but we shouldn't always expect things to go easy. It's evident to me that the devil is worried about our ideas, and he wants to stop them. So, whose side are you on?"

He looked round the room. Pete and Simon were

staring at him avidly; Helen and Avril were looking uncomfortable but agreeable; Martin and his glasses were nodding furiously and everybody else looked considerably challenged by Terry's words.

A girl called Sarah, who hadn't said much up until then got up and addressed the rest of them. "We can't be put off by such a small thing as Terry getting detention. So what? Maybe it will even attract a few of the people we want to invite! I'm not saying we should all go out and do something wrong to get folk to look at us ... but maybe we can turn Terry's disadvantage to our advantage!"

"Well said!" called out Martin, and the others clapped.

"Right!" announced Terry. "Let battle commence! This week I want you all to invite at least six people to the Christian Union. I know they won't all come, that's why I want you to invite a few each. And I think all we should do at that meeting, is introduce them to the C.U. We can tell them what we stand for and perhaps give a testimony of what Jesus means in our lives."

Martin interrupted ... "We ought to give them a chance to ask us questions as well. Even if we don't know all the answers, we should at least show that we don't mind having our faith debated."

"Good, right!" said Terry. "We'll end this meeting now, but can you come and tell me what you are prepared to do or say next Wednesday? Then I'll make up the programme."

Everyone got out of their seats and clustered round Terry, who was writing things down as fast as he could.

"Who are you inviting?" asked Pete to Martin.

"I'm not sure yet. I think I'd better pray about that

one."

"Well one thing is for sure," commented Pete.

"What's that?"

"We all know who Terry's going to invite ...!"

4

What Are You Doing Wednesday?

If you are a pupil, then detention is something you have to bear and the sooner it's over the better. If you are a teacher and you are asked to do detention duty — it's the biggest pain in the neck in the world. Most teachers find it annoying to sit and look after bad boys (and girls for that matter) but Mr. Bellamy found it impossible!

Terry and Bob sat behind desks near each other, but didn't dare say a word. It wasn't that Bob was scared of a wally like Bellamy, it was just that you knew very well that one remark out of place would keep you there longer, or even get you another detention. So they sat in silence, bored to tears, writing essays on unimportant pieces of English prose.

Suddenly it was all over. Bellamy looked at his watch and yawned. "All right you lot. Out."

There were only six of them, but they made enough row for you to think that a whole class was leaving.

"Not you, Ellis, nor you, Harris." Mr. Bellamy looked down his nose at them (and that was a long long way).

"I don't believe it, the toad!" whispered Bob to Terry.

"Just back off, all right?" said Terry, not wanting any more hassles than he had had already.

Mr. Bellamy stood in front of them in his sergeant major pose. "I hope you realise how lightly you boys are getting off? If I had been an ordinary member of the public, I might have called the police out to the street brawl of yours!"

Bob made a move towards him, but Terry put his elbow in his ribs.

Mr. Bellamy went on, "I don't want to see or hear about either of you in this vein again. Next time I would not be so lenient and that is a warning."

"Threat, more like!" grumbled Bob as they walked down the corridor. "That bloke's really got it in for me."

"Yes, well," replied Terry, "he doesn't seem to like me much either."

They walked along in silence for a few minutes.

"Er ... thanks for taking this so well," said Bob. "I think I owe you one, eh?"

"No, that's OK," said Terry, then he stopped. "Hey, there is one thing you could do for me — but only if you want to."

Bob was surprised. "I said I owed you one. What is it?" He couldn't imagine Terry asking him to beat someone up for him, and yet that was the only favour he ever got asked to perform.

"What are you doing Wednesday at lunch?" asked Terry.

"I never do nothing any day," replied Bob.

"Well, you know when I saw you down the shops? You said that you thought the Christian Union wasn't for people like you?" asked Terry.

"Yeh, that's right," answered Bob.

"Well, this Wednesday, we're having a sort of 'open meeting' for people who might like to come and just see what it's all about. How about i.?"

"Me? Me? At a Christian meeting?" began Bob, then suddenly he stopped as a crashingly brilliant idea came to his head. But of course! If Terry was involved in all of this, then it stood to reason that his sister was going to be there too! Brilliant! Bob's mind started working overtime.

"Why not?" Terry answered. "We're all asking people to come, so you won't be the only one there who doesn't normally go." (Come on, Lord! You can do it!)

"Wednesday you say?" mused Bob. "Wednesday, well maybe I will. I won't promise to be there, but maybe I will." And with that he laughed and made his way out of school, swinging his jacket over his shoulder as he went ....

Terry went home too. He was in a good mood. He couldn't believe that Bob had actually agreed (well, not outright, but as good as) to come to their meeting! He sauntered down the street putting his hand in his pocket to search for his house key.

Indoors tea was nearly ready. Ah yes, well of course, Terry had had detention and was late home.

"That you, Terry love?" sang out Mrs. Ellis.

"Yes, I'm home at last," shouted out Terry. Phew, what a day.

Mrs. Ellis came in, carrying a tablecloth under her arm and a tray in her hands. "Set the table for us,

Terry. How did you get on? Did that boy tell them it wasn't you?" asked his mum.

"No, mum," said Terry laughing. "It's hardly the kind of situation to start protesting in. Anyway, it's over now."

Carol wandered in, wearing a set of headphones with a cassette player on the end. She had one ear on and one ear off, that way she could listen to a record and still not miss anything that was going on.

"Hi, Terry. All right?" she asked.

"Yes, I'm fine," he replied.

"Please, please tell me now!" sang Carol and stood looking in the mirror, miming the rest of the words.

"Hey, Mum! Can Sharon come over tonight?"

"I don't see why not. Have you got much homework?"

"Yes, that's why I want her to come round. Mr. Wood gave us some stuff to do and we're allowed to do it together," she explained.

"Oh, Carol, I do wish you'd talk properly." Mrs. Ellis tried despairingly to get her children to lose their cockney accents, but it was hard work.

"Do you think Sharon's hair would suit her blond?" asked Carol to no one in particular.

"What on earth would she want to do that for?" asked Terry.

'Ah ha!' thought Carol. 'A reaction!'

"Why not? Don't you think it would look nice?" Carol retorted.

"I don't see the point of messing up your own hair, that's all. Anyway, she's got quite nice hair." Terry was talking just for the sake of it. He wanted to try and erase his detention from his mind for a while.

'Oh great!' Carol thought. 'We're warming up now!'

Terry carried on laying the table.

"She's not going out with Alistair any more," Carol said lightly.

"Who's not?" asked Terry straightening a knife.

"Sharon!" said Carol impatiently. "She's young and free and single now." She waited with baited breath for Terry's reaction.

He went through to the kitchen and brought back the salt and pepper pots.

"Well?" Carol was bursting with curiosity. Terry put the condiments down firmly and looked at his sister.

"Well what?" Honestly sometimes it was exasperating having a teenage sister. They talked in complete riddles and then expected you to understand what was going on.

"I just said that Sharon hasn't got a boyfriend any more, and you said how much you liked her hair!" To Carol it was all perfectly logical.

As the penny dropped, Terry shook his head.

"Carol, if you're asking me to go out with Sharon, there's a lot more to consider than just her hair! I'd be going out with the rest of her as well ..."

"So you do like her!!" Carol yelled triumphantly.

"Carol!" yelled Terry.

"Tea's ready," smiled Mum bringing in steaming plates of meat and two veg.

Carol looked over to Terry.

"We'll continue this conversation at a later date ... OK?"

Terry sighed and reached for the ketchup.

. . . . .

50

"Hi! What are you doing Wednesday? … No, that's not right … Hey! Is it Tuesday already? Have you heard what's happening tomorrow? … Good grief, that sounds worse!" Martin was looking into the bathroom mirror. He was trying desperately to work out a good line of patter to invite people to the C.U. meeting.

"I'm not very good at this. Who am I supposed to invite, anyway?" he thought. Ah well, he'd pray about that later, right now he had to rehearse.

"Have you ever wondered what happens in C6 on Wednesdays? … no … there's never anything to do here at lunchtimes — except Wednesdays that is …" Martin gave a huge sigh, and grabbed the bath towel off the rack.

"Ah well, perhaps it'll sound better when I've got my clothes on."

· · · · ·

Helen and Avril were chatting at Avril's gate.

"Who are you inviting, Helen?" asked her friend.

"I haven't a clue! I mean this whole idea of Terry's has gone a bit far — how can he expect *me* to mingle with yobs?"

Avril looked a bit worried at her friend.

"Come on, Helen," she said. "We really must try. Perhaps we could invite some people together? How about Sheila and her lot?"

Helen looked aghast.

"But her father works on a building site!"

"Yes, I know," replied Avril, "but we were reminded that Jesus didn't care about people's background, He just cared about people."

Helen was having a real hard time now, because she

knew in her heart that what Avril said was true — it was just all so embarrassing.

"All right. Sheila and her friends. Mind you, I'm only going to ask them once — and I'm not asking the one with pink hair!"

. . . . .

School the next day had an air of excitement about it for at least ten Christian kids. They had all thought seriously about the people they should invite. Some of them had even prayed about it. But this was it! The moment of truth! Would any of the people they had invited actually turn up?

Martin had managed amazingly well. He had bumped into some friends who were in his class last year (they had gone down this year) so he had told them all about the Open House meeting at the C.U. They looked mildly surprised but nodded and said they would try and remember. From there he had walked into the school football team (for which he was a reserve), and had managed to hold their attention long enough to make his announcement. Their reaction was pretty good, there were a few shuffles and smirks, but nothing like he had expected.

But Martin's greatest achievement was with Tracey Burton (he fervently hoped Terry wouldn't mind). He had seen Tracey looking at the C.U. posters on the noticeboard. He came up behind her and said, "Hello, Trace! Fancy coming to our meeting then?"

Tracey spun round, eyes wide with surprise (she was good at that).

"Oh, Martin! You frightened the living daylights out of me!"

Martin laughed. "Sorry! I saw you looking at the posters. Good, aren't they? It was Terry Ellis' idea."

Tracey thought for a moment, and then asked, "Terry Ellis? He'll be there then? At this meeting?"

"Will he be there?" laughed Martin again. "He'll be leading it!"

"What room did you say it was in?" The eyelash batting was in full swing now.

"C6," replied Martin. "Lunchtime today. See you there then?" Martin was getting all hot under the collar — he was amazed at his own courage!

"Yeh, why not?" replied Tracey.

· · · · ·

Sheila and her friends were not quite as easy to handle:

"Oh yeh, what's that when it's at home?" asked the one with the pink hair.

"C.U. stands for Christian Union," explained Avril. "We're having an Open House to show people what the C.U.'s all about."

"My life! That sounds boring!" retorted Sheila.

"How do you know if you've never been?" asked Helen. (She hadn't meant to get involved, but Sheila got up her nose rather quickly.)

"Why should we want to know about that, anyway? It's all about God and stuff, it's hardly exciting, is it?" said Sheila.

Helen looked put out. "Why don't you come and find out? … Scared?" Now they were all interested. Sheila's crowd gathered round, looking from Helen to Sheila and back to Helen again.

"Course I'm not scared! Who could be scared of a

stupid load of idiots talking about God?" Sheila was going slightly red by this time.

"See you there then, 12.30 OK?"

Helen and Avril left, hair flouncing and swaying in a way that said 'We won!'

"Well done, Helen!" chanted Avril. "I really didn't think you'd ask them!"

"Nothing to it," replied Helen. Her knees wouldn't keep still and she thought she might pass out at any moment.

Meanwhile, Bob was having a struggle with his conscience. The last thing he wanted to do was to go to this meeting thing, and yet on the other hand ... it was such a good way to get to know Carol a little bit better. I mean, she was bound to be there, being Terry's sister and that. Also, somehow he didn't want to let Terry down. Normally, he wouldn't give a fig who he let down, but Terry had treated him differently. Not only had he got him out of a scrape, but he hadn't told on him in the head's office. It was almost as if Terry didn't see him as the same bloke that everyone else saw. He was Bob the all right-type of bloke, not Bob the rebellious troublemaker that everybody avoided. He spoke to Bob as if he were normal!

'So, now, here I am kicking a can round the yard at school, wondering what to do,' thought Bob.

"Bob!" a rough edgy sort of voice yelled out at him. He turned round. It was Nick Turner and gang.

Nick was a big bloke, but unfortunately his brains didn't match his stature. He was a troublemaker but in a different way to Bob. Nick was getting on for stupid; he was very easily swayed and for this reason he was a useful instrument for Bob to use.

Bob, on the other hand, was clever, and he used his cleverness to outsmart people. He planned things — and right now he was making plans for this lunch-time meeting.

"Hey, Nick! How's it going?" he smiled.

"All right, I s'pose," replied Nick. "Me and the lads was on the look out for a bit of action."

Bob laughed to himself. Nick and his lads wouldn't know 'action' if they fell over it! Aloud he said, "Well, I know just the place for you! Follow me!"

'What a stroke of luck,' thought Bob. 'This is the perfect disguise! If I go in with this mob, I won't be noticed as an individual.

"What's going on then, Bob?" asked one of the others.

"Just wait and see!" There was no way he was going to let them know where they were going!

5

The C.U. Meeting

C6 was a normal size classroom with desks, chairs and a blackboard. It also happened to be the R.E. room which meant the walls were plastered with posters of Hindu rites and Jewish Laws and sometimes things about Christianity as well. There's not a lot you can do with a classroom to make it look good, but the C.U. members had moved the desks about so that people could sit on them. They did it in a sort of horse shoe shape, the idea being that everyone could see and hear what was going on.

Avril shivered. "Brrrr! I must admit that I'm a bit worried about this. Say no one comes?"

"Say everyone comes??" said Pete. "What on earth will we do if everyone we've invited turns up? It must amount to around sixty people — we wouldn't get them all in!"

Terry looked round the room.

"It's a bit quiet in here. We should have had a cassette playing in the background somewhere."

Martin brightened. "I've got a small one in my case! I'll go and get it." Really he was just relieved to get out of the room — the tension was getting unbearable.

At 12.15 when Martin came back with the cassette player and a few tapes, he was surprised to see only twelve people in the room.

"Don't worry!" said Terry. "It's early yet ..."

And even as he said it, there was a clatter of feet and the door burst open as the girl with the pink hair pushed her friend through the door. This was followed by giggles and remarks of "You go first ... it was you that wanted to come! ... There's nobody in there!" After even more pushing and shoving, Terry went over to the door and grinned at them.

"Come on in, ladies, no need to be afraid! Find yourself a seat."

He was met by a dubious glance from Sheila and then they all trooped in. Martin immediately turned up the cassette player and everyone relaxed. Before Sheila's crowd could make any more remarks, some more people came in. Quite an assortment they were, some Terry didn't recognise. 'Great!' he thought. 'If I don't know them, then the other members have done a great job in inviting people other than their friends.'

One person he did recognise was Tracey Burton. He had to admit to himself that he was a little surprised to see her there. He had never thought of her as being the slightest bit interested in anything spiritual. 'She's so ... so ... (actually the word he was looking for was 'attractive' — but he pushed it from his mind!) well, independent and sort of carefree, not very deep,' thought Terry.

The room was filling up nicely, although a bit noisily. Terry glanced at his watch. They were five minutes late in starting, perhaps they should begin. It was just that he didn't like to start in case there were more to come —

like Bob Harris, for instance. He had to admit to himself that it was a bit embarrassing when the person you had invited yourself hadn't turned up — especially when it was your stupid idea in the first place!

'Ah well. On with the show,' thought Terry. Aloud he shouted, "OK everyone, can I have your attention, please?"

He was amazed when they stopped talking and turned their attention to him. He cleared his throat.

"Hmm, yes ... well ... thank you all for coming. We didn't expect quite so many of you, but it's great to see you all the same. Now, the idea behind this meeting is to introduce you to the Christian Union, to explain what goes on here and hopefully you will find it interesting enough to want to come again. For those of you who don't know ... my name is Terry Ellis." He was very aware of everyone looking at him, especially Tracey who seemed to have developed a twitch in one eye. He loosened his tie.

"Er ... right ... well, the C.U. is not just for Christians. We like to think that it is for anyone with questions about God, or who maybe just wants to know the facts of being a Christian."

"Ere! What's all this then??" The door had opened and the shaven head of Nick Turner had peered round the corner.

"Oh push off, Nick!" yelled Pink Hair.

This request was met with a few more in a similar vein as Nick, Bob and four other lads kicked their way into the classroom.

"Watchit, mate! I'm sitting there!" said one of the gang as he pushed Martin off the top of a desk. Martin held onto his glasses and looked furious. He gave Terry a look that said 'I told you so' and found another seat.

"Come in and find somewhere to sit, lads," called Terry as cheerfully as he could. "Anywhere will do."

"Now, as I was saying. The C.U. is for everybody, and I mean that. It matters to us that everyone is given a chance to know about Jesus." ... A desk went over, spilling its contents absolutely everywhere. Bob laughed out loud and everyone turned round and glared at him.

"Leave it, don't worry," said Terry, trying desperately to regain attention.

"The first item we would like to present to you is Avril who is going to tell you how she became a Christian."

"That's daft!" shouted Nick. "We're all Christians! We were born in a Christian country. So Avril is going to tell us how she was born! Ha! Ha! Come on then, let's have the gory details!!" Nick's gang joined in the cheers.

Avril stood up. "I'm going to tell you how I became a Christian." Bob burped. He was fed up now. It was obvious that Carol didn't come to this type of thing, otherwise she would have been here by now.

Avril was losing her patience, so she picked on Bob.

"Do you know Jesus, Bob?" she asked.

"Not personally! Ha! Ha! Get it? You said did I know Jesus, and I said 'not personally'! Ha! Ha!" Bob fell about laughing at his wisecrack.

"Well, perhaps we can help you find Him," she said with a superior air.

"Don't worry, Avril — I'll try and find him meself!!" he said, and promptly started opening all the desk lids and crawling underneath the chairs shouting out,

"Jesus! Where are you? Come on, show yourself!" He then proceeded to crawl out to the front of the class where Avril was and looking up he said to her, "Nope! Sorry, Avril, he appears to have pushed off!"

By now, half the people in the room were laughing with him, and the other half looked like they were getting ready to leave.

"OK, Bob, you've had your fun." Terry was holding his hands up in an effort to calm everybody down.

"Carry on, Avril."

"That's funny!" retorted Bob. "I've seen most of the 'Carry On' films, but I've not seen 'Carry On Avril'!"

Avril was very red in the face and obviously didn't want to carry on in the least, but she took a deep breath.

"Before I was a Christian, I found the world quite a lonely place to live in ..." The room went dead quiet.

"Nobody seemed to really care and nobody ever seemed to listen to me, or try to understand my feelings. But once I discovered Jesus — well, it was like finding your very best friend ... it was ..."

CRRAASSHH!!

Over went two chairs. Once again the attention was turned from Avril to Bob.

"WHAT A LOAD OF CODS!" yelled Bob as another chair followed the others. And then, to the astonishment of the rest of them, Bob made his way to the door, kicking over every chair, throwing anything and everything that got in his way at the wall. He started chanting, "What a load of Rubbish!" which was quickly taken up by the other yobs and they marched out chanting and slammed the door behind them.

The room went totally silent. Avril and Terry were left standing at the front. There were two broken chair legs lying by his feet on the floor.

Slowly a few people got up and picked their things off the desks and left.

"Oh come on, you folks!" yelled Terry. "Give us a chance!"

"Sorry, Terry," said someone at the back, "but if a teacher heard that racket and comes in here — we're all for it. We'd better get out."

There was nothing they could do. The C.U. members just stood there and watched as all their plans and hard work walked out of the door.

. . . . .

It was two o'clock in the afternoon and Bob was in town. When he had slammed out of the C.U. meeting, he had also slammed right out of school. OK, so it was still lunchtime so nobody stopped him, but he knew he had no intention of going back for the rest of the day. His hands were thrust deep into his pockets and he felt mutinous. Normally if he was feeling like that he would smash a window and relieve the tension — but today was different. Today he just didn't know how he felt, it was such a mixture of emotions ... hate, envy, spite, sadness ... all muddled up with some kind of urgent longing.

He walked round town for the third time, trying hard not to analyse his feelings.

"What a load of cods," he repeated to himself. "How could I have ever been daft enough to even stay there long enough to listen to it? What was it she said? — 'It's like finding your best friend!' What a joke!" The trouble was that everything he had heard in that meeting was a bit too near the truth — nobody cared, nobody listened.

'And nobody ever will,' thought Bob. 'Where is the God that would have time for someone like me? It's all *rubbish!*' By now the hate and spite was rapidly being taken over by that sensation of longing.

It's a desperately horrible feeling, needing to be needed, wanting to be wanted, and seeing someone else grinning and saying, 'Look what I've found!' and knowing that all you've got is a dad who doesn't know you exist and a background full of trouble. Bob beat the air with his fist and out loud he shouted, "It's not fair!" The anger was rising and as he looked about him he saw the off-licence. He sorted out the money in his pocket and pushed his way into the shop.

"Ullo, Bob, how's yer dad?" The bloke behind the counter knew Bob's face straight off, he was often in here buying cans of lager for his dad. "How much is half a bottle of scotch?" asked Bob, not bothering to acknowledge him.

The man selected a few bottles of different brands and went into a speech on how much better this one was than that one etc.

"On the hard stuff, eh?" he said. He liked to have his little joke.

"Me dad's birthday," lied Bob, waiting impatiently for the man to wrap the bottle in that stupid tissue paper that you don't want anyway....

"Is it? Well, wish him a happy one from me!" he said, still smiling jovially as if the world were a wonderful place to live in.

"Ta," said Bob, snatching the bottle and making a quick getaway.

"Bye then, lad, tell him not to drink it all at once, eh?

Ha! Ha!" Hands on the counter he grinned and nodded until Bob had disappeared down the road. Then his expression changed and he shook his head worriedly. Bob lost no time in unscrewing the top and taking a large gulp of scotch. It caught fire in the back of his throat and he choked. But then he could feel the warmth spreading through his body and he started to relax.

Bob had this little hideaway. There were three derelict houses just round the back of the shops. One of them still had a roof over the front room so it was relatively dry, and when he wanted to be alone — away from his dad — that's where he went. So it was only natural that he should head for his hideout now.

In a way, that front room was more of a home to him than his own house. There was nobody shouting at him, he could think without being disturbed and at this moment he could get quietly drunk all on his own.

There are several steps to getting drunk — the idea being to blot out all the rotten things that have been happening to you. At first Bob enjoyed that warm feeling, it was almost like being hugged (his mum used to do that when he was little). It felt secure and cosy. He relaxed and leaned his head against the wall. He slid to the floor, smiling, 'I don't need them,' he thought. 'I don't need *anybody*. I'm all right on my own.'

He drank some more ... 'Fancy Avril telling us how she was born!' he giggled to himself. 'Anyway, she looks more like she was manufactured than actually born!' He laughed again.

"We showed 'em!" he yelled. "Me and the lads gave 'em what for! We rupdistered ... no ... we ruptured them ... no ... we *disrupted* that meeting!" This was followed by a few rounds of "What a load of rubbish!"

The lack of pronunciation showed that Bob was now losing control of his words. With half the bottle gone, he would soon lose control of his other senses, and if he kept on drinking, he would simply lose control, full stop.

After the giggles comes the depression.

"You think you're so great, God!" shouted Bob. "Sitting up there in heaven, you've got a cushy number, you have! Well what about me? What do you think it's like to be Bobby Harris, eh? What's the use of staying up in the sky when people need you down here, eh?" Tears started welling up in his eyes.

"It's not *fair*. None of it's *fair!* You get born with a load of problems and that's your lot. End of existence. Amen!"

After this little speech, he promptly fell asleep, the bottle somehow still upright beside him. He didn't wake up for ages, and when he did, he realised it was already late.

'Must be getting on for four,' thought Bob. 'I'd better go home before I'm missed.' He stood to his feet and the room went round at 45rpm. 'I'd better clear my head first,' he thought and downed the last quarter of the bottle.

One of the other effects of drinking that much scotch is that when the fresh air hits you — it tends to give you a variety of side effects. It was for this reason that Bob was marching along the road waving an empty whisky bottle in the air and singing 'Jingle Bells' at the top of his voice.

"Jingle all the way!!" He stopped. "Oh no! Flashing lights! I can't bear it when I get flashing lights."

Unfortunately for Bob, the lights were not directly

the result of his drinking bout, but more the result of a passing police car.

"All right, mate. In the car!" said a burly voice.

Bob felt an arm going under his armpit.

"'Ere! What's all this? Get off!" cried Bob.

"OK, Sonny. We've been celebrating Christmas a bit early this year, haven't we? I think you'd better come down the station and sober up."

He was pushed into a police car.

"Sober up?" cried Bob. "Are you incinerating that I'm drunk??"

"I think we can safely say that," replied the sergeant.

"You must be mistaken! You've got the wrong bloke!" explained Bob. "And you can turn those flashing lights off, they're giving me a headache ... in fact ... I think ... I'm going ... "

The other policeman quickly wound down the window and shoved Bob's head out just in time. ('Throwing up' is one of the other delights of being drunk.)

. . . . .

"Oh! Careful, that hurts!" Sharon frowned at her best friend.

"Sorry," murmured Carol. "But I've got to comb your hair through before we can try it another way."

The two friends were in Carol's bedroom, and they had turned it into a beauty parlour. Fortunately, it had its own basin and things, so washing Sharon's hair and then altering the shade (just subtly) shouldn't be too much of a problem. Carol's room was her castle — no one was allowed in without her permission — so they were quite safe to experiment, away from prying eyes.

They were having fun, sitting in front of the dressing-table mirror and putting their hair up, then pulling their fringes over their eyes, putting on horrendous-coloured lipsticks and laughing themselves silly at the results. This routine went on for about half an hour until Carol stood up and said very firmly — "Right!"

In between her fingers swung a packet of hair dye.

"Oh, Carol, do you think it's going to be all right?" Sharon looked very worried. (How on earth had she managed to let herself get roped into a stupid idea like this?)

"Nothing to it," replied Carol confidently. "We'll just follow the instructions on the packet, and your hair should be one shade brighter!"

"I thought you said Terry liked my hair as it was? Why are we doing this?" she asked.

Carol sighed. "Look, Sharon, he only said he liked it, he didn't say it was sensational or anything, and look at the competition! Tracey's hair is twice as thick as yours, and it's a beautiful shade of auburn. Yours is … well … mousey."

Sharon turned to the mirror again while Carol read through the instructions.

"Would you say your hair was medium or long?" she asked.

"I don't really know," Sharon frowned. "Why do you need to know that?"

"Never mind, we'll go for long." (The packet said use more if your hair was long, no point in taking chances.)

"What are you doing, Carol?" Sharon had now come across the room and was looking over her shoulder. There were times when Carol could really look as if she knew exactly what she was doing — even when she didn't!

66

"OK!" she ordered. "Sit here and keep your head over the sink."

The next thing Sharon knew was that her hair was getting covered in this horrible thick gooey stuff.

"Pooh! It smells terrible!" she mumbled from the sink.

"It's only the bleach — keep your eyes closed, we don't want any accidents." Carol was well into the hairdressing scene by now.

Sharon jerked her head up. *"Bleach!"* she yelled. But Carol caught hold of the back of her neck and pushed her down in the water again.

"Well, of course there's bleach in it! How do you expect to get your hair even one shade lighter if you don't use a mixture with bleach in it?"

Sharon's heart started to race. "I think we'd better wash it off."

"Don't be daft, it's only been on five minutes and the packet says to leave it on for at least twenty." (Well, for long hair anyway.)

To relieve the panic, Carol moved over to the record player and put on an album and they were soon singing along and doing their famous double act in front of the mirror. They were having a great time, with Sharon miming to "Careless Whisper" using a hairbrush as a microphone and trying to look glamorous with a towel like a turban on her head. Carol joined in playing make-believe guitar on her nightie case. They often did daft things like that.

It was a nice LP so they played it again and got very engrossed looking at the photos on the inside sleeve.

"Oh, no!" cried Carol. *"We've forgotten your hair!!"*

Sharon put her hands up to her turban.

"Good grief! How long has this stuff been on?!"

"Never mind how long it's been on ... let's get it off!" yelled Carol.

Suddenly her mouth had gone dry and she had visions of her friend with burnt pieces of hair coming from her almost bald head.

Sharon bent her head over the sink while Carol started rinsing off the thick gunge as fast as she could.

"Keep your head down, for goodness' sake, Shaz!" she shouted.

"I want to see it!" complained Sharon.

Under her breath Carol replied, "Oh no you don't!" She could hardly bring herself to look at the damage, so she flung a dry towel over Sharon's head and started rubbing furiously.

That was a bit too much for Sharon who was determined to see her hair, so she grabbed hold of the towel and threw it across the room — but just as she threw it there was a knock at the door.

Terry poked his head round and said, "Sorry to butt in, girls, but I thought you'd like to know that ... *what on earth*? ... Sharon ... your hair!"

"Get out!" screamed Carol and pushed him back through the door.

Sharon hadn't had a chance to look at her hair yet, so she just stood there with her hair almost albino white and said to Carol — "Do you think he liked it?"

6

Owning Up

The police car purred its way through town. It's funny how you don't realise how many people actually look to see who's in a police car — until you're in one yourself.

"So what's the problem then, son?" asked Sgt. Fraser.

"How do you mean?" replied Bob.

"Well, people don't usually get rip-roaring drunk in the middle of the afternoon, especially when they should be at school, at a rough guess. So there must have been a reason for you making that kind of mistake," he explained.

"It was no mistake," said Bob, feeling bold. "I meant to do it."

"Did you now?" replied the policeman. "Well, that's very unfortunate for you. Not only were you disturbing the peace, but you were wasting police time as well. At least if there had been a reason behind all this, we might have been able to understand better. However, have it your way ... drunk and disorderly plus wasting police time is quite a hefty charge."

Bob went cold. They were going to nick him! He was expecting a good talking-to and maybe even a cup of black coffee — but a charge? This called for desperate measures.

"You can't book me, I'm under age!" cried Bob.

"Oh dear, under age as well, eh? Perhaps we had better just take you home to your parents and explain what happened," said Sgt. Fraser.

'Oh no,' thought Bob. 'My dad'll go absolutely spare! I've got to get out of this.'

Aloud he managed, "It's OK, I can find my own way home, thanks."

"Where do you live?"

Silence.

"Where do you live?"

More silence.

"OK, drive to the station, nick him and then take him home."

"Look," said Bob, desperate to make some kind of deal. "There's only my dad at home, he won't be interested in coppers coming round. You'll only be wasting your breath. Give me a break?"

The two policemen looked at each other, then Sgt. Fraser said, "I think we'd better get you home, you're going green again. Where did you say your house was?"

. . . . .

Mr. Harris opened the door, expecting to see Bob and to give him a piece of his mind for being late a second time. The last thing he expected to see was two rather large policemen.

"What's happened?" Mr. Harris was white.

They pulled Bob from behind them where he had taken cover.

"Is this your son?" asked one of them.

70

"What's he done?" replied Mr. Harris.

"I asked you if he was your son, Mr. Harris?"

Bob's dad's eyes were darting from Bob to the police as he tried to sum up the situation. "Yes, of course he's my son. What's he done?"

"He was found wandering round town, completely drunk out of his mind," said Sgt. Fraser. It didn't take him long to sum people up, and he didn't like what he saw of Bob's dad. It was easy to see where the problem was.

"Drunk?" Mr. Harris tried to look surprised. "My son, drunk! I never heard of such a thing! Why would he do that, he's a good boy is my Bob."

"Give it a rest, Dad," said Bob. "Just let me come in and lie down, all right?"

"He wouldn't have got the booze from you by any chance, would he?" asked Sgt. Fraser.

Mr. Harris looked mad. "What do you take me for, letting a young lad like that get drunk! I'm an upright citizen!"

This wasn't going to get anyone anywhere.

"Right," said the Sergeant. "We'll let Bob off with a caution this time, but if we catch him doing anything … *anything* wrong another time, he'll be for the high jump. Understood?"

"Yes. Thanks." Bob was not about to blow this.

"Right," they both said and walked off down the path to the car.

As soon as they had gone, Mr. Harris threw Bob into the front room.

"Right! You've had it! I've tried with you. I've brought you up on my own and this is how you repay me. Well, do you know how I'm going to repay you?

71

Do you?"

Mr. Harris didn't wait for a reply, he just blacked Bob's eye again. Bob sat on the floor where he landed and glared at his dad.

"Yeh, that's all you know, isn't it? That's the only physical side of you I ever see! Go on — hit me again! Do you think it's gonna make the slightest bit of difference to me? At least that policeman had the concern to ask me *why* I got drunk. But not *you*."

Bob was pointing his finger at his dad. "It would never occur to you, would it? And if it did, you couldn't give a monkey's about me, anyway!"

There was a strange silence in the room, and Bob was aware that the only sound was the two of them breathing very heavily. And then Bob's dad came over to him, and said very softly ... "Is that what you think? Is that really how you see me?"

"Yeh," said Bob. "What's the point in shouting at me for getting drunk, when you're rarely sober yourself?"

"And when was the last time *you* asked *me* why that was?" asked his dad.

"What do you mean?"

"Life isn't one sided, Bobby. It doesn't just revolve around you and what you think and what you do, it revolves around other people, too. Believe it or not, I have an existence too, you know," explained his dad. Bob had never heard his dad speak like this.

"Never think I don't care about you," Mr. Harris continued. "I may have a funny way of showing it, like you said, but I worry like mad about bringing you up by myself."

"Why did she leave us, Dad?" asked Bob, not mentioning his mum by name, but knowing that Dad knew who he meant.

His dad gave a twisted smile. "The great W. Why? Where? What for? Who with? If only we knew the answers to all those questions." He looked at Bob. "I don't really know why. All I know is when she went, I didn't know what to do. I had you to look after and you were only small. So I just took to the bottle ..."

Bob didn't quite know what to say, he felt terribly sorry for his dad, and yet he could see himself becoming a younger version of him if he didn't do something about it soon. It had been such a strange week, this week, it was almost as if he were seeing himself for the first time. Those conversations he had with Terry about needing a friend and everything ...

"Do you believe in God, Dad?" asked Bob suddenly.

"Good grief, boy! What on earth made you ask that?" he replied.

"I just wondered, that's all."

"Well, put it this way. If there is a God, he hasn't been around this house in a long long time."

"Yeh, but I mean, didn't you ever wonder if you could change the life you live for a better one or anything?" kept on Bob.

"When your mother walked out, she took my life with her. She took my hope, my faith, everything. All I've got left is you and that bottle on the shelf over there," stated Mr. Harris.

"This bloke at school reckons that God can change your life." Another bald statement from Bob.

His dad looked at him quizzically. "Here, you're not becoming one of those religious maniacs, are you?

I'll tell you this now — I'd rather see you drunk! Don't you start coming home with funny ideas, me lad."

The tables were turning and Bob decided now was a good time to escape to his room. "Nah! Not me! Don't worry, mate, I got better things to do!" And with that Bob leapt up the stairs to his room.

Once he was sitting on his bed, he went over that conversation with his dad a hundred times. It was amazing, he had never ever really spoken to his dad — and he certainly would never have dared ask him why his mum left home and things like that.

'Maybe I've got him wrong. I haven't really looked at life from his point of view. This really is a very strange day!' he thought as he reached for the On button on his radio.

Music is very good therapy. Bob thought so, anyway. It could calm your nerves down and make you think clearer. He began to think again of the few short chats he had had with Terry Ellis. Whichever way he looked at it — he had to admit Terry really seemed to know what he was talking about, and yet to actually believe there was a God and that He was someone who actually cared for you — seemed a bit too hard to swallow. And like his dad had said ... all those unanswered questions. Why does God let people suffer? Why has he left me without a proper family? No, it didn't add up.

Bob got up and went over to the window. His room overlooked a busy street and he often just watched people as they went about their daily lives. Tonight as he looked he saw someone he recognised. Yes! It was Carol Ellis and her mate (that's funny, that's the second time he'd seen them round there). It occurred to Bob then that maybe Carol's mate lived near him ... although he wasn't at all sure she was the same mate Carol was with the other day, because this one seemed to have different coloured hair ...

. . . . .

"Then what did she say?" asked Carol, all ears.

"Oh, Carol, it was dreadful!" cried Sharon. "I've always got on so well with my mum, and I don't think she'll ever trust me again!"

Carol put her hands on her hips. "Oh come off it, Shaz!" she said. "It can't have been *that* bad!"

"No, it was much worse!! And just look at the state of my hair now!" she cried.

"I don't understand why she tried to dye it back herself. I mean, that's how we got into the mess in the first place! She should have taken you to the hairdressers' confided Carol.

This was probably one of the more sensible things Carol had said this particular week. When Sharon had arrived home from Carol's house on that fateful night, Mrs. Richards nearly had to be scraped off the ceiling, she hit the roof so fast. She had made Sharon sit in a chair and not move until she came back with a packet of shampoo-in hair colour which she had borrowed from her next door neighbour. According to the packet, the colour was 'Autumn Chestnut' and should have turned her hair a sort of reddy-brown, but Sharon's hair was *so* white to start with, that as it was only a tint and not a proper dye, it promptly turned poor Sharon's hair a pathetic reddy-pink.

"The worst thing," said Carol, "is that Sheila's

friend with pink hair is liable to think you're taking the mick!"

"Oh shut up, stop making it worse."

They slowly drifted up the road, chatting and looking in a few shop windows.

They hadn't realised, of course, that Bob was looking at them from his window. He watched Carol as she walked down the road and wondered again how he could get to meet her, and again he realised that Terry was his best bet. Perhaps it wouldn't be such a bad idea to have a chat with him again because, apart from Carol, there really were quite a few things that he wanted to ask him about.

The following day at school, Terry had been surprised when Bob had asked to chat to him again. Terry had just said OK, but they hadn't arranged a time or anything. It was weird, from where Terry was, to see Bob, because although he could swear that Bob wasn't a Christian or anything, he really seemed to be different. He was the same sort of lout he had always been and yet he somehow had a different kind of attitude. 'Silly really,' thought Terry. 'You spend your time praying for someone and then when they start behaving differently — you wonder why!' It was true that Terry had spent a great deal of time praying about Bob. Ever since they had met in the town centre Terry had sensed that Bob was really quite a desperate character and he knew that Jesus had specialised in changing people like him.

'I wonder what he wants to talk about?' thought Terry. 'Probably nothing to do with Christianity at all. He probably fancies my sister or something!' Terry laughed to himself at the idea.

It was break and Terry was on his way to the tuck shop. Martin caught up with him and when they had bought their crisps they spied Helen and Avril sitting at a table together.

"Oh dear ... do you think they'll ever speak to us again?" asked Martin.

"Want to find out?" challenged Terry.

They sauntered over and sat down opposite them.

"Oh, it's you," said Helen and continued unwrapping her chocolate biscuit.

"Yes," said Martin brightly. "Nice biscuits those."

Helen looked at him. "Well don't suppose for one minute I'm going to offer you one after the way you treated my friend!"

"The way I treated ...?" gasped Martin.

"Now, Helen, there's no need to get shirty. We all make mistakes," offered Terry.

"Yes," said Avril, talking for the first time. "But not always quite such enormous ones!"

"Listen, girls, I'm sorry if you're upset about the meeting, but really, when you think about it, the only thing that any of us really got hurt — was our egos. So we were made to look like idiots! So what! Jesus was made to look pretty stupid by his enemies now and again."

"You always have to make it a spiritual issue, don't you?" remarked Avril.

"That's not fair!" said Martin. "It *is* a spiritual issue!"

"Anyway, listen you three ... I've got some great news!" said Terry.

They all raised their eyebrows.

"Yes, you see I met Bob this morning and he wants

77

to have a chat with me! Isn't that great? After all the hassle and everything, he's still eager to talk!"

"Well, I heard that he's been eyeing your sister up and down, so you'd better make sure he's on the level," said Helen.

"No, I'm serious about this, folks! I think he really wants to talk and I'm going to give him every opportunity to tell me how he feels," said Terry.

A chocolate-covered doughnut suddenly waved itself at them.

"Oh, here comes Simon," remarked Martin.

Simon and his cake made their way over to the table.

"Hi! What's new?" asked Simon innocently.

He was awarded Avril's best scowl and Martin's 'don't-ask' look.

"Listen, Simon," said Terry. "I've been having more conversation with Bob Harris ..."

"You mean you still speak to him?" said Simon in amazement.

"Don't you start as well, Simon, I'm having a hard enough time with everyone else. Look, all I want from you is some backing. It's no good me having a chat with Bob and taking him seriously if I can't rely on you lot to back me up."

"What exactly do you mean by back up?" asked Helen.

"Well," said Terry, "what I plan to do is to ask Bob to come round for tea or something, and then if he really wants to talk to me about Christianity, he will have the perfect opportunity afterwards. But I need to be assured by you lot, that if I then bring him to the C.U. meeting next week, that you will welcome him."

There was a bit of a stunned silence at the table, and you could almost hear everyone's minds whirring. Avril was wondering if you could ever forgive anybody for that much humiliation; Martin was figuring out whether there was a reading in the Bible that dealt with people pushing you off desks — and Simon was just working out a plan for getting invited round for tea as well!

"So what do you think?"

Simon put his cake down. "Is it worth going after one interested party at the risk of upsetting all the other people who came to the meeting? I know that Jesus said to rejoice when a lamb comes back to the fold and all that, but we don't even know if he's really interested or just having us on a lump of string, do we?"

"I don't mind giving him another chance." This was Avril speaking, and everyone looked at her in amazement. "The thing is, when I gave my testimony that day — I know Bob made all that disturbance — but I'm sure he was taking it in. You know how you can feel if someone is really listening, well I think he was. I don't particularly ever want to go through that scene again, but I think it is important that we give him the benefit of the doubt."

"All in favour?" smiled Terry.

Four hands went up.

"Great," he said. "I'll get on with it then."

· · · · ·

The last two lessons of the day were games. It was a combined effort with several other classes. It just 'happened' that Terry's class met up with Bob's.

There was a choice of activities. Running outdoors, badminton in the other gym, or a mini assault course in this gym. Both Terry and Bob chose the assault course.

"Hi," panted Terry as he climbed the rope beside Bob.

"Yeh," replied Bob. It wasn't the right answer but when you are swinging wildly with your leg caught round a rope, it's sufficient.

"Do you still want to talk?" Terry asked.

"AAAAh!" replied Bob as he burnt his leg sliding down again. "Yeh, there's a few things I wanna put straight."

Lifting himself between two bars, Terry started a routine.

"My mum's a good cook — why not come round for tea and ..."

"*Me*?" Bob sat on the vaulting horse and looked at Terry as if he had just spoken to him in Russian. "You want me to come round your house??"

"Yeh, I thought ... cor ... phew! ... hang on a minute ..." He untangled himself from the bars and sat on a coconut mat. "I thought it would be a good place to talk."

Bob leapt off the bars on to the floor beside Terry.

"I don't know, I'm not used to that kind of thing." Even as he said it, he could have bitten his tongue off as he thought of Carol! What a great opportunity to get to chat to her.

"Well, if you don't like the idea ..." Terry was saying.

"Er ... no ... it's fine, great, OK" muttered Bob. Oh good grief, what was he getting himself into?

A whistle blew. "That's it, lads! In the shower."

"Come round tomorrow, about half-five, OK?" shouted Terry as he ran with the rest of his class to the changing rooms.

Bob did a couple of press-ups as he tried to get some kind of plan of action together. This could be his big break with Carol — and yet on the other hand he found himself looking forward to his chat with Terry Ellis.

7

Tea at Terry's

"Are you in or out tonight, Terry?" asked his mum. It's not that she kept that kind of close eye on him, she just liked to plan her evenings according to everyone else's.

"I'm in," he said. "Oh, come to think of it, I need to ask you a favour." Mrs. Ellis was busy putting things away in the front room (trying to make some sense of the mess ...). "Hmm. That sounds interesting."

"Well, you know that boy Bob that I was telling you about? The one who messed up the Christian Union meeting? Well, I was wondering if he could come round to tea tomorrow night?"

Terry waited for the reaction. His mum looked mildly surprised.

"You want to invite round the boy who messed your meeting up? Not that it surprises me at all, they're all the same to you, aren't they?"

"Who are?" Terry looked puzzled.

"Birds with broken wings, half-drowned puppies, old-age pensioners and yobs like Bobby Harris." As she spoke, she went on tidying the room. There must be three days' worth of newspapers under the cushion, and she had never known anyone like Carol for accumulating half-bottles of nail varnish.

"Hey, come on! You make me sound like some kind of do-gooder. I'm only trying to help Bob see things a bit straighter," said Terry.

"Of course you are, love. And you know very well he can come to tea … I just hope he doesn't start kicking our furniture about, that's all. Anyway, how did you come to invite him round? I thought he wasn't speaking to you."

It's a very hard thing to explain to your mum, after all, as far as she knew, Bob was the fella who had got Terry a detention. He laughed. "Yes I know, it does all sound a bit confusing, doesn't it? But you know what it's like, Mum, when someone all of a sudden takes an interest in Christianity — it doesn't really matter what happened beforehand — you just want to help."

Terry's mum knew all right. Although she was a quiet woman, she was a terrific Christian and shared her faith with everyone she met. In fact, that's how she'd met Raymond Ellis, Terry's dad. He was a bit of a tearaway in his time, and she'd taken him under her wing. In fact, many of her best friends had become Christians because of her witness. So, yes, she understood Terry's feelings.

"Tomorrow you say?" she asked.

"If that's OK" he replied.

"Fine," she smiled. Unknown to Terry, she and Raymond had been chatting about Terry's involvement with this lad Bob, and they were just a bit worried. Good didn't always win over evil in this world, and it occurred to them that Bob could lead Terry into some very rough ways, so although they were prepared to allow their son to make friends with a rebel, they were keeping a rather close eye on the friendship. So maybe it was a good thing that Terry had invited him home, at least they would get to see for themselves what he was really like.

Meanwhile, back at Bob's house, things were very different. For a start, the only person who did any tidying was Bob! His dad was back to his usual drunken state and was sitting in his armchair in the front room watching one of those hideous quiz games they put on the telly in the late afternoons. Bob could hear the occasional grunting and growling as his dad joined in with the TV contestants. It was such a dull life for Bob, no one to talk to, nothing to do. It was no wonder he spent so much time walking round town.

"I'll be late coming home tomorrow," stated Bob in a flat monotone.

"No you won't. I want you here where I can keep an eye on yer. I don't want no police knocking on my door again. Hear me?" His dad turned back to the telly.

"I'm going round to a mate's house for tea," said Bob as if he hadn't heard a word Mr. Harris had said. He had expected his dad to be annoyed, because it meant he would have to get his own tea, and that would mean forfeiting watching TV for half an hour or so.

"I said, I want you here."

"Tough, this is important."

"What! What are you talking about?"

"I've got things to discuss, important things, and I'm going round a friend's house to sort things out."

All sorts of possibilities flew through his dad's head.

"Hang on, what do you mean, important? What's going on?" he asked.

"Nothing to do with you," retorted Bob. "I've got a life to lead, remember?"

Mr. Harris got up from the armchair. He was a large bloke, greasy and unpleasant and not the sort of person you would be cheeky to unless you really had to.

"Sort things out? What's going on? Oh good grief, you haven't got a girl into trouble, have you? Bob, you'll be the death of me! Who is she?"

Bob was not amused.

"Listen, Dad, nobody has got anybody into trouble, OK? I'm going round to see Terry, his mum's invited me there for tea. That's it. Full stop. End of story. Get it?!" There were times when his old man made him feel sick, and this was one of them. There always had to be an ulterior motive for anything you did. There always had to be something dodgy in the proceedings. Well, there wasn't, and Bob was determined to show him that his life and his dad's life were two separate things.

"So, for once in your life," Bob went on, "you'll have to get your filthy great body out of that armchair and make your own tea, because I won't be here to get it for you!" With that, Bob left the room.

His dad sighed and settled down in his armchair again. He couldn't make out what was going on with his son just lately. Getting into trouble with the law, and then all this talk about God ...

'The younger generation ... I dunno ...' he thought, and stared at the telly again.

. . . . .

Friday at school always had a kind of comfy feel to it. You knew that in just a few hours they would let you out and the whole weekend lay stretched ahead of you.

Kids always got noisier on Friday afternoons and the teachers had a job to teach them anything at all, although this was partly due to the fact that teachers liked Friday afternoons as well and felt the same way about it as the kids did. So this particular Friday was no different, apart from the fact that Terry's class had to have a different teacher for French because Mr. Holliday was away. So, just to make Friday complete the class were amused to find that they had to have Mr. Bellamy, the deputy head.

It was unfortunate for Mr. Bellamy because he didn't speak French and more unfortunate still because Terry's class knew it! It didn't help that Mr. Bellamy was probably the most unpopular member of staff at Brentons, and the kids saw this as a chance to play him up without getting into trouble.

"Please, sir!" shouted a curly headed girl. "I can't understand these verbs, could you explain them to me?" There were muffled giggles all over the classroom.

Mr. Bellamy coughed and said, "Good grief, girl! Can't you even manage a few simple sentences? Now sit down and get on with it."

More muffled laughter.

"Please, sir?" This time Martin joined in. "Quelle heure est-il?"

"Now look!" began Bellamy. "I understand that your work has been given to you and I will not have you disturbing the class! If you can't understand your French you will just have to sit and read quietly."

This kind of behaviour carried on throughout the lesson.

By the time the bell went, the kids were helpless with

mirth and Mr. Bellamy was in a foul mood. He realised that the kids were being deliberately ignorant and also that he couldn't retaliate without losing face, and he was determined to take it out on someone. So as the bell rang he shouted out, "All right everybody, put your chairs under your desks and get out of my sight ... not you, Ellis!"

It was so unusual for Terry to get pulled up for anything, that most of the class stopped what they were doing to stare at him.

"Come on, the rest of you ... out!" demanded Bellamy, and the class dismissed.

Martin went over to Terry and whispered, "I'll wait for you outside."

When they had all gone, Mr. Bellamy turned to Terry.

"Well, Ellis, I hear that you have been making trouble again."

Terry frowned, he couldn't think what the deputy head meant.

"How, sir?" he asked.

"I hear there was a disturbance at this Christian meeting you run."

"Oh that." Terry was quite relieved, after all, nothing much had happened.

"Yes that. Don't think I don't know what's going on. I'm not daft you know. It's the way a lot of trouble is organised these days," he warned.

Terry was amazed ... Trouble? ... Organised? ... What was he on about?

"I'm afraid I don't understand." It was a stupid thing to say, but he didn't know what else to do.

Mr. Bellamy folded his arms and glared at him.

"I am well aware that the pupils in this school are not over fond of me ... but I tell you this, I know when the wool is being pulled over my eyes. You and this other lad pretend to be enemies in the hope that you can then carry on making trouble together and no one will suspect. But not any more, Ellis! I'm on to you! I'm going to be watching you very very carefully — understand? And what's more I'm going to expose your little game to the head as soon as I get the chance!"

Terry was stunned. It was like something out of a movie! Mr. Bellamy *really* thought there was something sinister going on.

"All right, you can go now, but don't forget, Ellis." Mr. Bellamy was looking down on Terry as if he were something he liked to put his foot on.

Martin met Terry outside.

"What did he say?" he asked.

"Good question," remarked Terry. "He seems to have some bee in his bonnet about me causing trouble with Bob Harris. It's really strange, I can't quite make out what's going on."

Martin said in a small voice, "I think I can."

Terry turned to him. "How do you mean?"

Martin positioned his glasses and proceeded to explain with great confidence.

"Well, it's just like our minister is always saying. If you want to do something for the Lord, then watch out, because the devil won't be far behind, trying to muck it up!"

"Did your minister say that?" said Terry, looking surprised.

"Well, maybe not those exact words, but that's what he meant. Look, Terry, we've all been praying about

88

the C.U. situation and we've all been backing you with the Bob Harris thing — and look at the trouble we've had! Oh, I know Bob caused half of it himself, but there have been other things as well, like this trouble with Bellamy. Yes, I've no doubt that this is 'spiritual warfare', that's what it is!"

His friend thought about that for a moment. It was true what Martin had said, there was a lot of stuff happening. One minute Bob Harris was causing absolute havoc and then the next minute — he wanted to have a serious chat. One minute all the C.U. members were dedicated to the same cause and the next — they were all fighting like cat and dog. Maybe he was right.

"So, what do we do about it?" he asked.

Martin looked troubled. "Well, I can't remember all the sermon — but I think that praying about the situation is probably the best place to start. I'll notify the others."

"Good idea," commended Terry. "Oh, and by the way, get them to pray for me tonight ... you know Bob's coming round."

"Yes I know," replied Martin, looking even more troubled.

Back at Bob's house, Mr. Harris was waiting for Bob to come home. He had remembered that tonight was the night that Bob was going round to that Terry's house and something about it worried him.

He was very unused to Bob talking about anyone in particular, let alone quoting them, but the last few days it had been 'Terry says this ...' and 'Terry says that ...'. What kind of hold had he got on his son? He knew that Terry was religious in some way or other and it frightened him to think that Bob might be heading the same way. The other thing that annoyed him (although he wouldn't really admit it) was that he had never known Bob have respect for anyone — and he had always hoped that one day, somehow, it might be *him* that Bob turned to for advice and everything. So it was with mixed feelings that Mr. Harris greeted his son as he walked through the door.

"Didn't think you was coming home till later," he grunted.

Bob flung his jacket on the settee and replied, "Well, I've got to get changed, haven't I? I mean, I can hardly go round Terry's in school uniform, can I? Have you sorted out some food for yourself this evening?" This last question was put in out of concern for his dad (even though he was a pain, he didn't like to think of him starving while he was out).

"I'm gonna get meself some fish and chips later on. Here, what are you putting the immersion-heater on for?"

"I'm having a bath," stated Bob and went upstairs.

Mr. Harris sat back in his chair and looked puzzled. All of these actions were unlike Bob ... changing ... having a bath.... Then, all of a sudden, it clicked!

'A girl! There's a girl involved in this somewhere!' thought Bob's dad. Bob came belting down the stairs. "Here, where have you put my last year's Christmas presents?"

"Where have I what??" asked his dad.

"My presents, last year someone sent me some aftershave." Bob was getting very ruffled, he had to be at Terry's by half-five.

"They're in the sideboard with everything else — by the way, what are Terry's parents like?" his dad asked.

90

"I don't know, I've never met them. Are you sure it's in the sideboard?"

"Try the second shelf. So there's just him and his mum and dad then?" he asked.

"Yeh ... no, he's got a sister an' all. Ah, here it is, I hope that water's hot." Bob was a million miles away.

"Well you'd better hurry up else you'll be late." Mr. Harris concerned himself with the newspaper so that Bob couldn't see his face, and when Bob had gone upstairs, he treated himself to a chuckle.

"A sister, eh?" he laughed to himself. "I'm beginning to see the light meself, Bobby boy!"

. . . . .

At five o'clock, Terry was watching TV in an effort to think about something else.

"I hope this friend of yours likes sausage, beans and chips," said his mum as she made her way to the kitchen.

"Yeh, don't worry, I should think he lives on them," smiled Terry. He didn't know why he felt so keyed up about this. It was just that he had read quite a few books about rebels and tearaways becoming Christians and they had almost seemed like fairy stories, and yet here he was on the verge of seeing it happen (he hoped ... he prayed ...).

In fact, he had it all planned. Bob would arrive, his mum would like him, even Carol would get on with him, and then after tea Bob would ask Terry to explain more about Jesus and why Terry believed in him, and then Bob would understand and give his life to Christ right there in Terry's front room! This, of course, would only be the beginning — as naturally Bob would go back to school and convert every yob in the place and go on to become a great evangelist ....

"Mum!" yelled Carol. "Why are there five places set for tea? Who's coming?" She managed to observe and say all this without taking her eyes off her magazine, as she walked in.

"Oh, it's just a friend of Terry's" replied her mum.

Carol went white and stood in front of the telly so that Terry was forced to look at her instead.

"What's up?" he asked.

"Don't give me that! You've invited Tracey round for tea and you know full well that we don't get on!"

"Hang on ..."

"No excuses! How am I supposed to sit and look at her across the table? What if I'd invited Sharon round as well? Cor, Terry, sometimes you just don't think," she finished.

"And neither do you. As it happens I haven't invited Tracey round at all," he said.

"Oh," said Carol in a small voice. She felt rather silly now.

"To fill you in on the details, Bob's coming round for a chat, so I said he might as well come for tea. OK?" asked Terry.

Carol looked puzzled. "Bob? Bob who?"

"Bob Harris. You know, the guy I told you about who carved our C.U. meeting up."

"But why would you want to invite *him* round? He's a bit of a head case from what I've heard!" said Carol irritably. (Things weren't going too well. She thought she was in for a fight with Tracey, and now there was just this dumb bloke coming round.)

Terry got up. "I'll just take my homework upstairs,

then I'll be down again," he said to no one in particular.

As soon as he got upstairs, the doorbell rang.

"Answer that for me, Carol, there's a good girl," shouted her mum from the kitchen.

Carol was halfway to the door when she realised that it was bound to be Bob. She blushed, not really knowing why. It was annoying, blushing, even when there was nothing to get hot under the collar about. Really, she just wasn't used to boys enough to relax and talk to one. Boys were always after you (according to the magazines) and were only interested in asking you out and all that. They were not people you talked to.

She opened the door.

Bob stood on the doorstep and looked at her.

She stood in the doorway and looked at him.

"Er ..." said Bob.

"Er ... come in. Terry's gone upstairs to take his homework up there." It was the first thing that came into her head.

Bob stood in the hallway. He was wearing his best leather jacket, a teeshirt and some jeans he had ironed himself.

Somehow he looked enormous in their little hall, and Carol had to look up a long way to see his face.

She was quite surprised with what she saw. This bloke was vaguely good-looking. A bit rough and ready, but if you tidied him up a bit he could be quite nice really.

She blushed again as she realised they were both still stood in the hall looking at each other. The ice was broken by Mrs. Ellis who came bustling out and said, "Ah, hello love, you must be Bob, come in the warm, the telly's on and Terry will be down in a minute. He's just taken his homework upstairs."

Bob looked at Carol and grinned. "Yeh, I know," he said.

He went through to the front room and sat on one of their posh velvet armchairs. He felt very uncomfortable (not because of the chairs, but because he wasn't used to this kind of treatment). He stretched his feet out in front of him, and his Doc Martens were filthy.

'Oh no!' he thought to himself. 'I knew I'd forget something!'

Before he could worry any more, Mrs. Ellis came through with a mug of tea.

"I hope you like tea — I can do you some coffee if you like? Isn't it cold? Did you come far? Switch channels if the telly's boring."

And so she went on, not giving Bob a chance to answer, but he didn't mind, he was finding Terry's mum a treat to listen to. It reminded him of some very early days in his own life.

"Oh, sorry, I didn't realise you were here!" It was Terry, he'd had his record player on upstairs and not heard the doorbell.

"Watcha," replied Bob. He was beginning to relax now and feel at home.

"You've met mum, then?" Terry said by way of conversation. "Has Carol been down?"

"Er ... yeh, she answered the door."

"I expect she was frosty, she usually is with people she doesn't know. Don't worry about her, she'll gradually thaw," said Terry. Now that Bob was actually here, he wondered whether it had been a wise move. His mum was being ever so nice to him — but he had to admit that Bob didn't actually go with the furniture!

There were some voices outside, and then Terry's dad came in. He eyed Bob with suspicion.

"Hello, Dad! This is Bob, remember, I told you about him," said Terry.

'Of course!' thought Mr. Ellis. 'This is the young ruffian that Terry's determined to convert!'

"Pleased to meet you, Bob," he said at once. "I hope you've got a strong stomach, you know my wife's cooking has floored stronger men than yourself."

Terry heaved a sigh of relief. 'Great, I think he's been accepted!' he thought ....

Tea was a bit of a complicated affair, with awkward questions and even more awkward answers.

Terry's dad ... "What's your father do then?"

Bob ... "He's on the dole."

Terry's mum ... "Ah well, I expect your mum's pleased to have him home with her."

Bob ... "They're divorced."

Terry's dad (a bit too jovially) ... "I suppose you have to share all the housework then, eh?"

Bob ... "I do it."

At this point Carol became a life saver by knocking a bottle of HP sauce all over the tablecloth. Everyone jumped up to save getting a lapful and Carol got the giggles. After this little escapade, everyone seemed to get along fine.

After tea Terry's mum came through and said, "You'll have to excuse me, but I've got to go out. We have a bible study at church tonight and I'm supposed to be taking part."

The rest smiled politely.

"Do you go to church at all, Bob?" asked Mr. Ellis as

lightly as possible.

"No. I've never really been ... well, only to a funeral," Bob replied.

Carol was sitting in a corner looking furious. 'Why can't they just leave people alone?' she thought.

Bob didn't seem to mind all the questions and even offered some information himself now and again.

"Well, maybe you could come with us one Sunday. Just tell Terry if you want to give it a try, eh?" he smiled.

"Thanks," replied Bob. Although he could see they were trying hard to get him to church, they didn't mean any harm.

In the long run — Terry's chat with Bob didn't really happen. For a start, Carol didn't want to leave the room. For one reason or another, she seemed to be there and Terry didn't want to embarrass Bob by asking what he wanted to talk about, in front of his sister.

The fact that Carol was there didn't bother Bob, in fact, Terry was beginning to think that there was something in the rumour he had heard about Bob fancying Carol. So in the end they all sat in the front room and watched TV and played a few records, and unbelievably Carol didn't even mention Wham, let alone play their albums. She suddenly had a great desire to listen to heavy rock!

It was a nice enough evening, and when Bob decided it was time to go, Terry saw him to the door.

"Thank your mum for the dinner, won't you?" asked Bob.

"Oh yeh, OK," said Terry. He was feeling a bit down as he hadn't managed to talk to Bob seriously at all.

"Oh, by the way, we'll talk some other time. Do you

know the derelict houses behind the shopping centre?"

Terry's eyebrows knitted together. "Yes, I think so."

"Well, be there tomorrow at four, all right?" This was one of Bob's more polite invitations.

"Right, I'll be there," Terry said firmly and closed the door.

Once inside, he stood there for a moment.

Derelict houses? What was going on?

8

Panic!

Carol stood looking into the window of Brenton's best clothes shop. She eyed the new leather jackets with great longing, and then looked away as she saw the prices. In the reflection of the shop window she saw Sharon racing up the street to meet her.

She looked puffed and gasped, "Ooh, sorry I'm late, Carol, my mum made me hoover the front room before she'd let me out!" She leant against the glass.

"That's all right, you haven't missed anything," replied Carol.

Saturday in town was their day for eyeing up the local talent along with every other kid in Brenton.

"Micky Dallington has been past with that Lisa, and dozy Nick Turner is around with his mates ... but no one else much." Carol's voice sounded a little low.

"What's up, Carol? You sound as if you were looking for someone in particular," said Sharon.

Carol blushed. "No. No, I was just bored waiting for you to arrive. Let's go and get a coke at the burger bar."

As they walked, Sharon tried to find out what was going on, by making innocent sounding remarks.

"Has Terry said anything else about me to you, then?

I've hardly bumped into him at all lately and I've nearly worn that red sweatshirt out that you said he'd like."

There was no reply from Carol who was walking next to her in silence.

"Carol!"

"Oh, sorry, what?" she asked.

"I was just asking you about Terry," said Sharon infuriated.

"What about him?" she replied.

"Well. What's been happening?" Sharon asked.

"Oh nothing much. He brought Bob Harris round to our house last night," she said casually.

"Bob Harris!! Round your house! Good grief, Carol, what on earth does Terry want with a blockhead like him?" she asked.

"Oh, it's something to do with the Christian Union ... and anyway, he's not such a blockhead," retorted Carol.

"What are you talking about? He's a right wally ... he's always in trouble ... he's always getting detention ... he's never in anyone's good books ... he's ... he's ..." she stopped as she saw the look on Carol's face.

"Oh no — Carol! You can't possibly ..." she started.

"Can't possibly what?" asked Carol, trying to look innocent.

Sharon stopped walking, put her hands on her hips and said, "Carol Ellis, I refuse to believe that you could fancy Bob Harris!"

"There's the burger bar, let's get that coke, I'm dying of thirst," said Carol, walking straight ahead and ignoring Sharon's comments.

Sharon ran after her shouting, "Hey! Hang on, wait for me! I won't say anything to anybody — honest!"

At the same time in town, there were two policemen going on their rounds. Although Brenton wasn't the absolute end in violence, there was still need to keep the shopping centre 'under surveillance'. It was always the same with these new places. The councils made them look really attractive with the benches for tired shoppers to sit on and the plastic palm trees in the indoor bit to make you feel like you were on holiday. But as well as being used by shoppers, it was used by every kid in town who had nothing better to do on a Saturday morning, so for the two policemen it was an endless round of "Turn that radio down a bit, sonny, give the shoppers a rest" and "Hey you! Get down off that palm tree!"

This particular morning, they were discussing their duties.

P.C. Burns, the larger of the two, was going through the list.

"There's that faulty alarm system at the jewellers. Then there's been a spate of shoplifting in Woolies again and — oh yes, there's that schoolkid who got done for being drunk, I've got his name here somewhere."

"I know the one you mean," replied P.C. Brooker. "It's that kid whose dad has been a right pain — Harris, that's his name. When they took the lad home, his dad gave Sgt. Fraser what for and the next day Harris' son was walking round with a black eye. Yes, I blame the father for that kid's behaviour."

"Well anyway, we've got to keep an eye out for him, because he's been given a warning, so any more funny behaviour and we collar him," P.C. Burns replied.

"OK" said P.C. Brooker and they wandered off down the centre.

. . . . .

As the afternoon drew on, Bob Harris made his appearance in town.

Unfortunately Carol had gone home by then, and so missed seeing her new heart-throb. Bob had bought himself a packet of cigarettes. He didn't know if Terry smoked — he didn't think he did, but he wasn't going to get caught out without any if he *did*.

He made his way to his hideout and found that he was about an hour too early. That was OK, it gave him time to think before Terry arrived. He had been doing a lot of thinking lately and had come to the conclusion that if Terry really had found a God that cared ... well, he'd like to hear a bit more about Him. But he felt totally ridiculous talking about it, so this hideout meant that he could talk to Terry without anyone else ever having to know about it.

He tried to remember all the things he was going to ask.

How do you know God's real?

What has He ever done for you?

Why should He give a fig for someone like me?

Why hasn't He helped me before now?

As Bob thought about these things, he began to feel angry about this God, who if He was there, could see the kind of life he led, and yet hadn't done anything to help him. 'What's the use?' he thought.

At around quarter to four, Bob took a walk outside his den to see if Terry was around. He hadn't told him the specific place because he didn't want everyone to know where his hideout was — so he had to make sure he spotted him when he arrived. The outside was a

101

dump, literally. It was full of old bits of broken furniture and piles of bricks, some assorted empty bottles and general rubbish. He had only found the place by accident when he was running away from a rival mob. He'd belted down this alleyway and come across the houses, and leapt into the nearest one. Then he adopted it for his own, even to the extent of clearing it up a bit so that he could live in it if he needed to. There was still a three piece in this one, and a table, so it wasn't such a bad place. A dark head appeared running down the road. 'Ah good!' thought Bob. 'He's here.'

"Watcha, Bob." Terry grinned, hoping it was the right thing to do. He was still a bit worried about all this — why did Bob want to meet in such a grotty place? He hoped there was nothing shady going on.

"This way," grunted Bob. It was strange how, even when he wanted to be friends, there was always that feeling of holding back, as if all good things would be taken from you in the end.

He led Terry to his 'House' and pointed to an armchair. Terry sat down on it (hoping he wouldn't catch anything) and Bob sat opposite him on the other. They sat in silence for a few minutes, as if they were summing each other up (which they were in a way) and then Bob offered Terry a cigarette.

"Wanna fag?" he asked.

Terry felt a bit awkward. He wasn't sure what to do. There was no one around to see them, but then again maybe this was all part of a trap! If Terry didn't take a cigarette then Bob would either think he was a wimp — or it could be that he wanted to see if Terry would stick to his principles. On the other hand, if he *did* take one, Bob would probably think that he was just the same as

102

all the rest and that his faith didn't count for much.

So he refused.

Bob eyed him cautiously and lit up. He waved the match in the air and threw it onto the floor. Somehow, smoking gave him the courage he needed to talk to Terry — it was like having something to hide behind.

"OK," he began. "Tell us about your God."

Terry was totally flummoxed! What now! Here! He couldn't think how to begin or which way to put things!

'Lord!' he prayed under his breath. 'Help!'

Aloud he said, "What do you want to know?"

Now it was Bob's turn to forget what he wanted to say. All those questions he had ready for him — where were they now?

"I dunno," he said. "Tell me why you believe in God, I suppose."

Terry thought for a moment, then he said, "I know that when Avril spoke at the C.U. meeting, it touched a raw nerve ..." Bob went to interrupt but Terry waved his hand at him.

"I know it did, because I can remember the same thing happening to me. It wasn't the same raw nerve but it was there just the same. You see the reason it hurt was because God wants you to know that he really does understand. If Avril had stood up and talked about how God had healed her little sister — it might not have meant too much to you — because you haven't got a little sister who's ill. But God obviously knew that you needed him as a friend and so he let Avril speak about it."

"You mean, God told Avril what to say?? How?" Bob was leaning forward now, trying to take in what Terry was saying.

"God speaks to people in various ways, and I can't say how he spoke to Avril that lunchtime because I don't know. Sometimes you can be reading the Bible and it might say 'feed the hungry' or it might say 'heal the sick' or in your case 'comfort the lonely'. And maybe Avril had read that just before she spoke, and felt that God wanted her to put that point across."

"All right, but I don't understand why God should bother. What's in it for Him?" asked Bob.

"It's more like what's in it for you," Terry replied. "When God put us on the earth, he gave us a choice. He said, 'All right, you can go my way, or you can go your own way.' Needless to say, man found it very hard to keep up with God's standards so he started going his own way. I mean, at times, it's easier to lie your way out of something than to tell the truth! It can be easier to do what everybody else does than to do what you think is right. See?"

Bob nodded.

"Right then, once you've started to go your own way, you start walking away from where God is and you become guilty of disobeying God's law," Terry said.

"How can you be guilty?" asked Bob. "You said it was our own choice."

"Yes it is!" replied Terry. "But it's still wrong or right. If you stay on the right side of this country's laws, then you're OK, but if you decide to disobey the laws, then you pay the penalty."

"Great, so now not only have I carved up my life in this world, but I haven't got a chance in God's world either!" Bob frowned and lit another cigarette.

"Maybe that's how it seems," said Terry. "But the whole idea of Christianity is that you can't save yourself. Christians are basically people who have said, 'Look, Lord, I've carved it up and I can't make it on my own.' And then it was up to God to work out a plan so that we didn't have to be punished for disobeying His law."

"So there's a way round it then?" Bob brightened a fraction.

"Yes. Because God decided to deal with us in a very special way. He decided to send His son Jesus down to earth. The reason behind this was that Jesus was perfect, He had never done anything wrong, so He had to be used as an example to us all," explained Terry rather badly.

"But I thought He died anyway?" said a bemused Bob.

"Yes, He did! But because He had never done anything wrong — He didn't *stay* dead! It was like sort of proof that dying is only a sort of semi-permanent state of affairs. There is a life to be led after we die, and if we decide we want to spend it in heaven then we have to ask God to let us in ... and if we decide we want to spend it in hell ... then we're idiots!" stated Terry.

"But you said that if you choose to go your own way, you can't go God's way, so how come God will let us in?" Bob seemed to be following the conversation very closely, picking him up on everything.

Terry was beginning to feel quite exhausted and was desperately trying to answer his questions fairly.

"That's a good question," he said. "You can picture what you've just said by imagining that you are on one side of a huge gap and God's on the other ..."

"That's exactly how it feels at the moment," put in Bob.

"Right! So now imagine a bridge going right across from you to God. Only instead of it being a real bridge — imagine it being Jesus!" said Terry triumphantly. "It's like Jesus is the way to get to God. So when you ask Jesus to get you to God, it's easy. He just lays down and lets you walk over him! He took your punishment, see?"

"That sounds terrible. What did Jesus ever do to deserve us walking over Him like that?" asked Bob.

"That's the point, you see. The only person who could take away all the things you had ever done wrong, was someone who had never done anything wrong himself. And that was Jesus. He died instead of you," explained Terry. "It was a sacrifice, but He was willing to do it, to save you having to be punished. So there is a way out and it *will* cost you something, but remember it cost Jesus *everything*."

Bob sat back in his armchair and tried to take in everything that Terry had said to him. It all sounded quite unbelievable and for some unknown reason it gave him a sort of knotted feeling in his stomach.

"I don't know ..." he sighed, and threw his fag end at the settee. Suddenly the whole atmosphere changed as the settee burst into flames!

"Terry! Quick! Help us! Bring that mat over here!!" yelled Bob in confusion. Terry grabbed the mat and dashed over to the settee where the two of them started to beat the sofa furiously.

The smoke was everywhere and getting thicker. They started to choke, but kept on beating.

"It's no use!" yelled Terry. "It's getting worse!" Even as he said it, the rug in his hands caught fire.

"What are we going to do??" shouted Bob above the

106

pandemonium.

"Get out! Fast!!" screamed Terry. The smoke was rising upwards and there was very little space left to breathe in. The fire had now caught hold of both armchairs, and a pile of newspapers.

"Run! Get out!" yelled Terry again. It was impossible. The smoke was so thick he couldn't even see Bob now, all he could hear was the sound of coughing and choking and in his bewilderment he didn't know if it was coming from Bob or himself. It was at this point he realised he didn't have any idea where the door was ... he had never been there before.

"Over here!" shouted Bob's voice. "Terry! This way!"

The pair of them were panic-stricken and the room was growing immensely hot. Terry just dived for where the voice had come from and suddenly found himself in moderately fresh air.

The next few minutes were a bit of a blank, and then they were aware of shouts and people and sirens.

"Sit down, love, you'll be all right in a minute," said a woman's voice.

"Are they burnt?" asked a child's voice.

"Here, it's that Bob What's-his-name! I bet he started it on purpose!" cried a third voice.

Terry and Bob sat on the ground letting all the confusion go over their heads. The world was still spinning a little and everything was slightly muzzy. Bob looked over at his friend .... "You all right?" he said.

"Yes, I think so," said Terry and promptly threw up. The smoke was still thick in his lungs.

The next thing they knew was that comforting sound of a voice of authority.

"All right, all right. Let us through. Well, what's been happening here then?"

Bob thought, 'It must be the firemen ... no, hang on, they'd be putting the fire out. It must be the police — oh no! Not twice in one week!' He was wrong, as it happened. The men who fought their way through the crowd were ambulancemen and before they knew what was happening, they were both stretchered into the ambulance and whisked away to Brenton Casualty.

It was after this event that P.C.s Burns and Brooker came sprinting down the alleyway in the direction of the fire.

"Typical!" said one bystander. "They spend all day walking round that precinct, but they're never here when you need them! You've missed it all, mate! The fire's out and the kids have been taken to hospital."

"What happened?" asked one of the policemen .

"Two schoolkids started a fire in that old derelict house, and then they couldn't get out in time to run away, I reckon," said the bystander.

"Schoolkids? What did they look like?" P.C. Burns said.

"Just like schoolkids look like on a Saturday, I suppose. Jeans, jackets, you know the kind of thing," he replied.

Another man pushed himself to the front. "One of them was that Bob What's-his-name. You know, his dad's a bit of a boozer."

"Bobby Harris?" asked P.C. Brooker. "Is that the lad you mean? Who was the other one?"

"Yeh, Harris! That was him. I didn't know the other one ... bit smarter, dark hair," he said.

"Right! Leave it to us!" The determined chin of Ernest Brooker stuck out half a mile, as he saw a 'highly commended' report in his reach.

"Come on, Burns! Brenton Casualty!" And with that they left the scene.

Terry and Bob were not badly hurt in the fire and so they were allowed to sit up in the ambulance. They looked at each other in confusion — what was going to happen now? They had both heard people in the crowd assuming that they were up to no good.

"They're never going to believe us," said Bob. He was shivering and rubbing his arms. The shock was setting in now and he was beginning to feel rough.

"Depends who 'they' are, really. I mean, my parents will be on my side, they know I'd never be daft enough to set a building on fire on purpose." He ran his hands through his hair. "Phew! Everything smells of smoke."

The ambulance came to a halt and they were both escorted into casualty. It was probably a good job they couldn't see themselves, because they looked like a pair of kids from Oliver Twist days when everyone had soot in their hair and nowhere to live. Their clothes were ruined as they had tried desperately to put out the fire, partly torn from the mad dash to get out and filthy and singed from their efforts with the rug. Altogether they looked awful.

"And what's been happening here?" asked a jovial doctor. (Why do they always ask such obvious questions?) Before either of them had a chance to say anything, one of the ambulancemen cut in.

"They were caught in a fire in those old derelict houses in town. Playing with matches probably," he stated.

This remark made both of the boys very angry. It

made them sound as if they were both about eight years old and irresponsible, whereas in fact it had actually been an accident. Well, maybe Bob shouldn't have been smoking in the first place, but they certainly had no intention of causing trouble.

"All right," said the doctor. "Let's have you in those cubicles, we'd better give you the once-over."

They protested, saying they were fine and could go home, but the medical staff insisted they were properly checked.

Sitting in the cubicle, Terry all of a sudden realised that his parents wouldn't know what was going on! He had to phone them; they would have a blue fit if they found out through someone else!

"Can I use a phone?" Terry asked somewhat timidly. Nurses and doctors always looked so forbidding with all those stethoscopes and needles and things.

A nurse came over and smiled at him. "Don't worry, you can phone your folks in five minutes. You both seem to be OK so we won't keep you in. Will your parents be at home?" She was very nice and Terry relaxed thinking it was all over.

However, when the curtain was pulled back they were met by the spectacle of Burns and Brooker the famous police duo! Bob and Terry froze. "The nurse said we could go home," offered Terry.

"I'm sure she did, sonny, but we want a word first. We need statements from both of you and there are a few questions to be asked," said P.C. Brooker confidently.

"I have to phone ..." started Bob, but he got no further as P.C. Burns interrupted.

"No need, Harris. There were witnesses at the scene

of the crime who told us who you were, and both sets of parents are waiting for you ... at the station. So if you'd like to get your bits and pieces together, I think a ride in a police car might do you both some good."

The boys stood rooted to the ground in astonishment.

"Here! What do you mean 'scene of the crime'? We haven't done anything wrong!" Bob yelled at them.

"Now there's no point in raising the roof, we'll get it all sorted out down the nick. Now let's go!" said P.C. Burns firmly. And they were marched out to the car.

They sat in the back in bewilderment. Neither of them felt very well and they just didn't need an ordeal like this at the moment. In fact, they both just wanted to sleep for a million years.

Bob looked at Terry with resignation and said, "Where's your God now?"

9

The Nick

Parker was from C.I.D. He had had a hard week and was just about to go home when he was told about the fire.

"They'll need questioning, sir," said an officer.

Parker sighed and resigned himself to the fact that he was the only one around available to do the job.

"All right, wheel them in," he said, and sat back in his swivel chair to await the young thugs.

The officer brought Terry and Bob in and left immediately.

The room went dead quiet as they stood there with this C.I.D. man summing them up.

"Well?" he asked abruptly.

Neither of them answered. Terry was thinking about all the TV series he had seen where you don't say anything until you've seen your lawyer ... but when you are still at school you feel a bit of a wally demanding a lawyer ... anyway he didn't have one. Bob's mind, on the other hand, was racing. He was remembering the warning the police gave him after his drunken bout and was sure he was in for borstal.

"All right, seeing as you seem to have forgotten how

to speak, perhaps I could ask you a few questions, like what were you doing in that old house?" he queried.

It was Bob that spoke up first. "I often go there. It's just somewhere to go," he offered.

"It's trespassing, laddie," was Parker's answer. "So you go there often. Well, what made today so special that you thought you should burn it to the ground, eh?"

"It was an accident!" blurted out Terry, and then realised how futile that sounded.

"Do you know how many times a week I hear people say that? 'It was an accident — I didn't mean to hit him … It was an accident — I didn't know the gun was loaded …' Can't you come up with something better than that? OK, back to the beginning. The two of you were in the house. Why?" he asked.

"We wanted to have a chat," said Bob.

"And we didn't want anyone else around …" put in Terry and again realised that everything he said sounded worse than he meant it.

"Oh? And why was that? What kind of secrets are you keeping from the world, eh? Had some plans to put together, did you?" Mr. Parker was fed up and hungry and he knew that Mrs. Parker would be annoyed because he was late, and his dinner would be cold. Why didn't these young lads just confess they set the place on fire, then he could go home.

"Look," said Bob. "We went there for a private chat, nothing sinister, OK? While we were there, I dropped a fag on the settee and it caught fire. We did our best to put it out — as you can see by our clothes — and that's all that happened. Like Terry said, it was an accident."

"So in short," said Parker, swivelling on his chair, "You were trespassing in a house, smoking under age and causing the fire service, the hospital and the police a lot of hard work." He sat and stared at them, twiddling his fingers (which was a thing he did a lot while he was trying to decide what had to be done).

Terry felt terrible. The whole thing had started out so innocently, and yet here they were in a lot of serious trouble — he hadn't even realised that it was trespassing. Even so, he didn't think there was any harm in it.

"So, I think we had better have statements from you both in separate rooms and then we'll take it from there." He reached for the internal phone. "Burns, come in here and get these statements sorted out." He looked up. "Your parents aren't going to be very happy, are they?"

... Mr. Harris and Mr. and Mrs. Ellis were very far from happy as they sat in the waiting room. It had been a most awkward situation as they hadn't met before, and so they had to introduce themselves.

"Er ... you must be Mr. Harris, I'm Raymond Ellis and this is my wife Pauline," said Mr. Ellis quietly.

Mr. Harris was very unsure how to react. Do you say 'pleased to meet you' on an occasion like this? And anyway, until he heard for himself, he wasn't entirely sure who was the guilty party, so he just nodded and grunted.

The waiting room was cold and stark. There were the usual posters warning you to watch out for thieves, and asking if you had an alarm fitted on your car. The chairs were hard and the room was painted in that regular sort of grey and green that they use in social service offices and the like. It was a sort of hopeless room. It made you feel as if *you* were the one that had done something wrong.

Pauline Ellis cleared her throat and said, "You'd think they would have a heater in here on a day like this, wouldn't you?"

Both men nodded. It was the kind of statement that women make and men ignore. In fact the only reason Mrs. Ellis had said it, was because she was worried sick about Terry.

"I don't suppose you know what happened at all?" ventured Mr. Ellis to Bob's dad.

Mr. Harris stopped looking at the posters and turned to him. "I haven't got a clue, apart from knowing there was a fire and neither of them were hurt. I think the police are trying to turn it into something bigger ... you know what they're like."

The three of them all returned to their own thoughts and sat staring at the walls. After a while Mr. Harris said, "My Bob's been talking about your Terry quite a bit lately. Been round for tea an' all, hasn't he?"

"That's right," replied Mrs. Ellis. "He came round last night."

"Funny that," muttered Mr. Harris.

"What do you mean?" asked Mrs. Ellis.

"Well, Bob's never been in any real trouble and then he makes friends with your lad, and this is the second lot of trouble he's been in." Mr. Harris was careful not to look at them when he said this.

"Are you trying to say that our Terry is behind this?" Mr. Ellis looked annoyed and insulted.

"No, I'm not saying anything, it's just funny that's all," he replied. "He's a bit of a churchgoer an' all, your son, isn't he? I know Bob's mentioned it ... I'm not so sure it don't put funny ideas in your head. You know, you read of these people going weird and sacrificing animals and all that ..."

"Mr. Harris, Terry is a Christian — not a religious maniac or a devil worshipper — I don't think you'll find they were burning sacrifices to unknown gods in that derelict place. I think you'd find if you met him yourself, that Terry is a very stable likeable lad."

"Well, I must admit that when Bob tells me about him — he does sound OK," he said.

"I can't think what's going on in that office," worried Mrs. Ellis. "What on earth could have happened? Why doesn't someone tell us something? Raymond, you'll have to find out because I'm not convinced that they are well enough to stand up to all this."

Mr. Harris was surprised. It seemed to him that Terry's parents were concerned about both boys, whereas he had only been concerned about Bob and tried to use Terry as the one to land the blame on.

"Shock can be a nasty thing," continued Mrs. Ellis. "They're supposed to be wrapped in warm blankets and drinking hot tea, not sat in a cold police station. I mean, if all they want is a statement, they could have come round to the house!"

Mr. Ellis consoled his wife. "Look, love, the Lord knows what's going on, we can't do anything about ourselves. We prayed before we came out, so let's just leave Him to sort it out, eh?"

Pauline Ellis tearfully agreed. "I just wish I knew what was happening, that's all."

Mr. Harris looked at himself. 'Why don't I feel like that?' he thought. 'I'm more concerned about myself than anyone. Bob's in the nick and I'm wondering who's gonna cook me dinner if they keep him here.' He scratched his head. 'I don't look after him very well.'

"Are you all right?" Mrs. Ellis looked concerned. "Perhaps I can get us a cup of tea?"

"No, don't worry," he replied. "I suppose I'm worried an' all, really."

The waiting was endless. They sat in the room for an hour and a half while the police took the boys' statements, checked them against each other and went back over the same questions hundreds of times.

"Would you like to come this way?" A policewoman appeared in the waiting room and led the boys' parents to another room where cups of tea were laid out on a bare table.

"Help yourselves. Someone will be bringing the boys along in a while and then we can get sorted out."

"And I wonder what *that's* supposed to mean?" said Mr. Harris.

They helped themselves to tea — more out of something to occupy them than anything, and then the door opened and a policeman came in, followed by Bob and Terry. Mrs. Ellis gasped, they looked awful in their smoke stained clothes and smudges of soot on their faces.

"Terry! Bob!" She ran over to them both, then turned round to Mr. Ellis.

"I'm taking them home. I don't care what anyone says. They can come back later ... they're all in!"

"It's all right, Mrs. Ellis," said the P.C. "They can go home now anyway. C.I.D. have done with them for now and you'll be hearing from us shortly with any results of their statements."

It was stupid really, but they all just stood and looked at each other. No one made a move.

"Right!" said Mr. Ellis. "Mr. Harris, perhaps you'd

like a lift in the car with Bob ... or perhaps you had better come round for tea and we can have a talk." Someone had to take charge of this, so Terry's dad thanked the police and then hustled everybody outside to the car.

When they got back to Terry's house, Carol tore the door open and flung her arms round her brother. She was not normally a very demonstrative person, but on this occasion she had been so worried about him.

"Terry! What happened? Are you all right?" And then she saw Bob standing by the gate. She could hardly fling her arms round him — but at the same time, she was tremendously relieved to see him on his feet.

"Carol, let us in for goodness' sake! These boys have had a terrible shock and need to rest," said Carol's mum.

Carol made way for everybody, and that included a man who she guessed must be Bob's dad.

"I'll put the kettle on," she volunteered, and ran out of the room, grateful to have time to think.

"Now I know you'll think I'm over-protective," said Mrs. Ellis, walking into the room with an armful of blankets, "but you are both just to sit in those armchairs with these round you and have a hot drink before you say another word. Raymond! Let them come round a bit first."

"Mum, you can be as over-protective as you like!" said Terry, putting the blanket round his shoulders. "Thanks for giving us a break."

All this time Mr. Harris had been watching the scene, and a lump had formed in his throat. It was mainly because he knew he would never have handled the situation like this, and he was more than grateful for these warm people around him. He decided against trying to do anything, and sat on the sofa and waited. After a few minutes, Carol arrived with the tea and they all busied themselves with the sugar and biscuits.

Soon they were settled, and Mr. Ellis said firmly but gently, "OK, lads, let's have it from the beginning."

Between them Bob and Terry pieced together the tale of how Bob had wanted to talk to Terry but they needed to go somewhere private. Bob then put in the bit about how he always used that derelict house anyway, and Terry said that he had agreed to meet him there.

The smoking came as no surprise to Bob's dad, although it raised eyebrows with the Ellises. It was hard to explain how the settee just whooshed into flames before they could think — and they both started getting very worked up telling how the smoke and flames nearly had them.

"All right, all right, calm down. Now ... have you told the police everything? You've told the same story there? You didn't try and protect each other or anything daft?" asked Mrs. Ellis.

They both shook their heads. They knew they were in enough hot water without making it any worse.

"Well, in that case I suggest that I drive Mr. Harris and Bob to their home and I'll deal with Terry when I get back." Terry's dad looked more disappointed in his son, than angry.

"That's good of you," said Mr. Harris and helped Bob to his feet.

While they were gone, Carol had a chance to chat to Terry on his own. "You frightened me silly. The police came round here and told Mum you'd been in a fire and that you were in hospital, and then they took Mum and Dad down the station. I just had to sit here till Mum phoned and said you were all right."

Terry looked at her. "I owe a lot of people apologies. Sorry, Cas, I just wanted to talk to Bob."

Carol smiled at her brother. "Yeh, I know. Hey, do you think Mum and Dad will still let you go around with him? They might ban him from the house or something."

"I shouldn't think so," replied Terry. "It was as much my fault as his. I was in agreement with the meeting ... and it did cross my mind that it might have been trespassing, but I didn't think it would matter really. Honestly, Carol, you should have been there — I thought we were going to get roasted alive! It was horrible. I've never prayed so hard in my life."

"Nor have I!" said Carol. "There are times when God really puts you to the test, and it certainly made me think very hard about my faith, I can tell you!"

Terry was very chuffed with what his sister had said. She had never been an out and out Christian, but she had never denied it either. Maybe she needed this kind of challenge to sort her own Christianity out. Maybe all this had happened for her — and not for Bob like he'd thought....

Aloud he said, "Well, I'm glad some good came out of it. I wonder how Bob will cope with his dad? I've heard he's got a rotten temper. I hope he doesn't take it out on him."

As it happened, Mr. Harris was going very easy with his son. He had seen so much happen in the last few days and now he wasn't sure whether he should shout at

Bob like he usually did, or perhaps try and talk to him like he knew Mr. Ellis would with Terry.

He decided to try and have a chat.

"Well, Bob, is there anything else to tell me?" he asked, a bit too roughly.

"Like what?" snapped Bob, unable to talk to his dad any other way.

"Come on, I'm trying to understand, give us a chance. Did anything else happen? Was it just that your fag fell on the settee ... or what?" said Mr. Harris. This wasn't going very well.

"There's nothing else to tell. It was an accident. It happened just like we told you before. Me and Terry was having a chat about God and that, and the settee caught fire. That's all," said Bob.

Mr. Harris tried changing the subject slightly.

"They're nice people, them Ellises, aren't they? I had quite a nice talk with them in that police waiting room."

Bob looked up, surprised.

"Did you really like them then?" he asked. He had been wondering how to approach a certain subject.

"Yeh, 'course I did. And they explained a bit more about their church and that." He sniffed. "Seems all above board."

"Well, I'm glad you think like that, because as it happens, I'm going to church with them this Sunday," Bob said casually.

If you had hit Bob's dad with a brick you couldn't have had more impact than that last statement.

Mr. Harris got to his feet. "You're doing WHAT?"

"I'm going to church with them this Sunday. They asked me if I'd like to go when I was there the other day.

Don't look like that, Dad, I'm not robbing a bank …
I'm just going to a church service!'

Bob's dad didn't know what to think. He was, as he'd
said before, worried about Bob turning into some kind
of religious nutter — but surely it had to be better than
having him wandering aimlessly around town.

Before he could answer, Bob spoke again. "Look,
Dad, this is my chance to find out some things for myself. If there's nothing worthwhile in Jesus, then I'll
leave Him alone. But if, like Terry says, I can have a
chance to start again … then I want to have that
chance."

These were big words for a fifteen year old boy, but
he meant them very sincerely, and his dad could see
that.

"All right. Give it a go. What harm can it do?" he
said. Not that Bob wouldn't have done it anyway, but
he felt he should sound like he had some authority over
him.

To his amazement, Bob grinned. He didn't do that
very often, and Mr. Harris decided that it suited him!

"Thanks, Dad," he said.

He'd never meant that before.

10

Sunday

Terry bumped his head on the sloping bit of ceiling under the stairs as he went to answer the phone.

Carol came racing up. "It'll be for me ... Sharon said she'd ring tonight." So Terry handed the phone over without answering it.

"Sharon?" said Carol.

"No, it's Bob," came back the reply. Poor Carol went several shades of maroon and said, "Oh, sorry, hang on, I'll get Terry."

"That's OK," he said, "you can take a message if you like. Just tell him that I'll take him up on his offer and meet him for church tomorrow, all right?"

Carol was still trying to get over the shock of talking to Bob and went silent for a moment.

"Hello? Are you still there?" said Bob, a bit puzzled.

"Oh, yes, fine. I'll tell him," said Carol, trying desperately to think of something else to say to keep him on the phone a bit longer. She needn't have worried.

"Carol, will you be going as well?" he asked.

"Oh yes, of course!" she answered in a rush. Good grief, she hadn't been to church in weeks! She always meant to go but her bed was so comfy on a Sunday morning.

"See you there then," he said and put the phone down.

Carol sat under the stairs for what seemed like hours trying to analyse the meaning behind the few words Bob had spoken to her. Was he just being polite, or did he really care whether she would be there or not? Ah well, either way she thought she'd better go and wash her hair. She was just going up the stairs when Terry caught her.

"Was it Sharon then?" he asked.

"Oh, sorry, Terry, no it wasn't — it was Bob. He left a message to say that he will meet you for church tomorrow," she repeated.

Terry was over the moon!

"You're kidding? He's actually going to come? Wow, brilliant!" He took hold of Carol and waltzed down the passage with her. They both laughed and acted stupid ... but for different reasons.

When she got up to her room, Carol sat on her bed and tried to reason with herself. 'Carol,' she thought, 'I don't know if I approve of you going to church just to catch a fella. In fact, no. I don't approve.' She started to brush her hair ready to wash it. 'Maybe,' she said to herself, 'Maybe, I've been waiting for the right opportunity to go back. If you don't go to church for a while and then you go back ... everyone looks at you and you can feel them thinking things about you. Some of them ignore you as if you've done something terrible, and others are so over-nice that it's just as embarrassing. In all honesty, I'd like to go and give it another try ....' As she spoke to herself, she began to realise that she was in fact praying. She was reasoning with Jesus about the things that worried her.

"Lord, help me to do it right this time. I know I have an ulterior motive for going to church — but at the same time, I do want to go for the right reasons too. When I thought something had happened to Terry and Bob, I realised how short life can be and I know I'm missing out on the best life by not sharing it with you." She ran the taps and began to prepare to shampoo ....

Downstairs, Terry was phoning Martin. Martin didn't actually go to the same church as Terry, but he would be dead chuffed to know that Bob Harris had finally decided to risk a church service with Terry.

"Hello, Martin?" he asked.

"Oh, hi Terry! How are you feeling? I heard about your accident. I bet that's put you off Bob Harris for life, hasn't it?" said Martin quite happily.

Terry was very put out.

"Honestly, Martin, sometimes you can be very annoying. The reason I'm ringing is the total opposite to being angry with Bob." Terry left a little gap in the conversation (for effect) and then announced, "Actually, he's coming to church with me tomorrow!"

The statement had the required effect. There was stunned silence on Martin's end of the line, then a gasp and he said, "Tell me that again. No, don't! Are you really saying that after all you've been through with that fire ... and not to mention the disaster at the C.U. meeting, you're actually going to walk into church with him?? Terry — he'll destroy it! If you didn't get your fingers burnt today, you're definitely in for a burning tomorrow. My advice is — don't do it." All this was firmly spoken from Martin.

Terry gave a resigned sigh and said, "Listen, Martin.

Don't you see the way God has worked this out? It's obvious that I had to go through all that, and Bob did too so that God could bring Bob to a place where he *really* had to acknowledge that he couldn't handle life by himself," explained Terry.

"I don't know," replied Martin. "You've been saying this all along, and it seems to go from bad to worse ... you said the C.U. chaos was all done so that God could talk to Bob. Now you're saying the same thing about the fire. Are you sure the devil's not just taking you for a ride?"

It was very exasperating trying to convince Martin that the only person who had the devil on their back was Bob, and that this was just the kind of 'spiritual warfare' that they had been talking about only the day before.

"Martin, I am totally convinced that this is God's plan and not the devil's. Hey, and even Carol has been touched by all this," he added confidently.

"Ah yes, but word has it that Carol's sweet on Bob anyway."

Terry decided he would give up this conversation as it only seemed to be driving a wedge between Martin and himself.

"Tell you what, why don't you just help by praying me through this, OK? And I'll give you a ring tomorrow and tell you how it went."

Martin sounded relieved. "Right. I'll wait to hear from you ... but Terry, be careful, OK?"

"Cor, you sound like my dad!" laughed Terry.

"Thank you and goodnight!" Martin laughed back and put the receiver down.

On Sunday morning Bob came downstairs in his

usual jeans and tee shirt and started preparing breakfast for himself and his dad.

Mr. Harris came in looking like someone who had just got out of bed. He was scratching his head and yawning and dying for a cup of tea.

"You're up early, Bobby, couldn't you sleep or something? I only came down because I heard the kettle go on."

Bob poured him a cup.

"The service starts at half ten, so I had to be up in time. I'm meeting Terry on the corner of Shepherds Road at ten." He poured himself a cup of tea and then helped himself to a slice of toast.

"Service? Ah yes! I'd forgotten all about that. It's your big day then, eh, Bob? ... Here! You're not going to church dressed like *that* are you, lad? It's not proper. I remember when we was little, we had to dress up in a proper shirt and tie," his dad said.

Bob carried on munching his toast and combing his hair at the same time. "Things are different today. Terry says for me to go how I feel comfortable, and this is it. He doesn't dress up or anything, he says that God only has a look at what's inside your heart — not what's on your back."

Mr. Harris shook his head. "Terry says ... Terry says ... you're beginning to sound like a parrot."

Bob shot his dad a glare.

Mr. Harris laughed. "No, there's no need to look like that. I was only joking. Is there any more toast going? Do us a slice before you go, there's a good lad."

"I won't get there at all at this rate!" mumbled Bob. "And how many times have I told you not to put the butter in the fridge? It's like a blooming rock."

"Aw, go on, go on. I suppose I can do me own toast for once. Just get back in time to put the dinner on, all right, son?" he replied.

Bob didn't need telling twice. He had his jacket on and was out of the house like a shot.

He ran most of the way and then slowed down just before he got to Shepherds Road — he didn't want Terry to know he was eager! As he walked along he spotted a few blokes he knew and nearly froze as they came over to him.

"Watcha, Bob! You're out early for a Sunday? Got a football match on?" one of them asked.

"I'm in a hurry," said Bob by way of excuse and pushed them aside and carried on walking. As he walked he thought, 'Tremendous, what a great start! I can't even get the guts to tell them what I'm really doing!' And with that, he turned round and ran back up the street and stopped them again.

He caught hold of the biggest one by his lapels and snarled, "I'm going to church. Wanna make something of it?"

The bloke gulped and stammered, "No. No, Bob, I was just passing the time of day, know what I mean?"

Bob let him go and walked off down the road.

Terry was waiting when Bob got there. They were both early, but not very bothered because there was quite a lot to say. Terry was worried that Bob might not like his church, he had been trying to see it from a stranger's point of view, and now he was getting edgy about it all.

Bob, on the other hand, just wanted to ask if there was anything he should know. "The only service I ever went to, you had to stand up and sit down every two minutes. I hadn't a clue what was going on," he explained.

Terry smiled. "Don't worry, it's not like that here. The minister will explain exactly what's happening."

Bob was relieved to see that Terry had a pair of jeans on too. He didn't want to look out of place. This was important to him and he was only going to give it one stab.

Terry realised that Bob was nervous so he said, "Look, they're a really great crowd and nothing like you are imagining. It'll be like falling off a log!"

They turned a corner and the church loomed up in the distance.

"No wonder I couldn't picture it," said Bob, "it don't look nothing like a church!"

That was true enough. It looked like a cross between an office block and hotel reception area. There were enormous glass windows so that you could see straight through to the foyer-sort-of-area, and people were milling around chatting and looking like they were at a wedding reception rather than a Sunday service.

There must have been over a hundred people standing around in that area, and as Bob saw them, his stomach tied itself in knots.

"There's a lot of people in there," he stated, swallowing hard.

"Yeh," replied Terry. "It's pretty easy to hide yourself in that lot. That's only a few of them ... we get a regular three hundred on a Sunday morning."

"*Three hundred??*" cried Bob. "Never!"

Some girls came rushing out of the church shouting hello to Terry and nodding at Bob. They certainly didn't look at him curiously, more sort of friendly than anything.

Before he knew it they were inside the building, joining the crowd, and Bob could now see the attraction as another young girl came up to them with a tray of coffees.

"Do you take sugar?" she smiled. "Hi, Terry, this your friend?"

There were basic introductions and Bob could feel someone's eyes boring into the back of his jacket. He turned round and found himself staring at Carol.

He nodded and she grinned at him. Then she came over and joined in the general chat with the others. Mrs. Ellis came up and spoke to Bob. "I take it you'll be sitting with us? I've saved you a seat in between Terry and Carol, I hope that will be all right?"

"Great! ... er ... I mean ... fine, thanks, Mrs. Ellis," replied Bob.

After that they all seemed to drift into the church and take their seats. The organist had already started playing something that sounded to Bob like 'I Do Like To Be Beside The Seaside', but turned out to be something called a 'chorus'. It was weird as people gradually joined in singing ... a bit like they did in a pub ... as they all picked up the tune and sang along. Bob felt a bit of a wally as he didn't know the tune or the words.

"Look up on the wall," suggested Terry.

And there, to Bob's amazement, the words of the song were flashed on to the wall by means of one of those overhead projector efforts. So, although he felt much too embarrassed to sing along — he could at least look at the words (or even mime to them!) and feel more a part of the service.

The church was filling up now and it was getting very confusing as half of them were singing and the other half were still saying hello to each other. Bob was watching it all go on with great interest. Then suddenly a man came to the front and started to welcome everybody to the service. He was a youngish fella with fashionable clothes and a spiky haircut. He was speaking through a mike so that everyone could hear him. Bob thought to himself, 'Must be one of the church members announcing the arrival of the vicar.'

"Who's he?' he asked Terry in a whisper.

"That's Alan, he's one of our ministers,' replied Terry.

One of them? That sounded strange to Bob. It was strange enough that this bloke was a minister anyway, but apparently there was more than one of them!

"How come you've got more than one minister, then?" asked Bob.

"Well, with over three hundred people, you need quite a few people to run it," he said.

The minister was telling them to stand up to sing another one of these choruses, and this time the organist was joined by three guitarists, a girl playing a flute, a bloke on bass guitar and a drummer! The music engulfed everybody and they all sang as if their lives depended on it! Bob just stood there looking from one person to another and wondering if he had come to the right building after all.

Terry nudged him. "You OK?" he asked.

"I'm a bit out of my depth at the moment. I can't take it all in — it's nothing like I expected. I didn't think you could sing to God like this!" Bob looked like a little boy at a fair for the first time. He just didn't know where to look first.

After the rousing chorus session, the minister stood

by his mike again. "It's great to see you all here, and I know there are quite a few of you who are here for the first time. I hope that you will be able to relax and enjoy worshipping God with us, but first, let's take some time to greet each other. Try and find someone you don't know and welcome them in the Lord. Now, I know you can take a long time doing this, so I shall limit you to three minutes!!" The congregation laughed and started to disperse around the church.

So just as Bob started to get a little used to the service, he found himself shaking hands with hundreds of people, all asking the same questions, but all being very friendly. He had been aware that the back of the head of the man in front looked slightly familiar and when he turned round, he recognised him straight away.

"Sergeant Fraser!" he said, startled. Sgt. Fraser shook hands with him.

"Hallo, lad, I heard you had made friends with young Terry. Good to see you here," he said.

"But ..." began Bob.

"No buts ... I hope you enjoy the service!" he laughed and went on to shake hands with someone else.

Bob was stupefied. No wonder he'd recognised the back of his head ... he had looked at it all the way to the police station that time when he was drunk!

Terry turned round and saw Bob's face.

"Yes, I should have told you he came here, but seeing as we didn't see him when we were interviewed about the fire — I didn't think it was worth mentioning. But looking at your face, I gather you have already met!"

Bob gulped. "Yeh, you could say that. He arrested me for being drunk and disorderly in the middle of the afternoon!"

They both saw the funny side and had uncontrollable fits of laughter.

"OK, everybody!" shouted the minister. "Let's find our seats again."

The service went on in much the same vein, with everybody getting excited every time Jesus was mentioned and there was much hand clapping and even dancing, when the choruses were sung.

Then someone stood up and prayed.

This had a profound effect on Bob. He had never heard anyone pray without reading it from a book, and this bloke was really going at it! "Lord!" he prayed. "I can never thank you enough for the day you found me. How did I ever manage without you? I know now it was something I should have done years ago, but these last two years have been the best years of my life and I am eternally grateful to you, Lord. Amen."

'That's funny!' thought Bob. 'He's an old bloke and yet he's only been a Christian for two years ... and I thought it was too late for me!'

More people prayed and Bob listened hard. Although the music was obviously attractive to him, it was these prayers that really got to him. Hearing people just pray out loud and express their feelings in such a public way was just unheard of. They were from all walks of life, these people, doctors, policemen, shopworkers, housewives, blokes on the dole ... he knew this by listening to them as they prayed about various situations in their lives. Amazing!

Bob Harris felt a lump come into his throat ... 'Good grief!' he thought, 'I can't handle this!'

But before he had any more time to think, the minister came back to the front and started to preach.

It was a good sermon, very listenable-to. He told them about Jesus calling his disciples for the first time and how he told one of them to put his net down in the lake. Apparently this bloke had been fishing all night and caught nothing, but Jesus told him to do it ... so he did it. He lowered his net and caught so many fish that he had to get all his mates to help him haul them on shore. Then Jesus told him to leave his nets and the fish and follow him. So the bloke did, because Jesus told him to.

Then the minister looked up and said, "And what has Jesus told you to do? Maybe what He has asked of you sounds strange ... it did to the disciples, but Jesus told them to do it, so they did, and found that whatever Jesus tells you to do is going to be for your benefit."

He looked around his congregation, and although he wasn't looking at Bob, Bob still felt that the words were going right through him. "Perhaps Jesus is asking you to give your life to Him, and you are refusing because it doesn't seem like the right time. Well look, friend, it didn't seem like the right time to catch fish — but it was! And if Jesus is telling you that the time is right to come to him — then it is! Don't put it off! Now is the time of salvation!"

They were very potent words and Bob felt that he knew exactly what that disciple had gone through. It was easy enough to say, "Yeh, I believe what you're saying is right ..." but it was another thing to put your money where your mouth was.

"Let's pray for a moment and consider what the Lord has said to us this morning. And while we have quiet for a few minutes, let us confess to Him what we should be doing. Remember, 'Jesus told him to do it ...

so he did it!' Listen to His voice and respond." The minister sat down and the church went very quiet.

Bob knew he had two alternatives. He could either ask Jesus to take over his life — or he could sit there and burst with the effort of ignoring Him.

"OK, Lord, you win." Bob prayed for the first time in his life. "But I don't know how to handle this at all, you are going to have to take me every step of the way."

Suddenly he was aware of music playing and for a blind moment of panic he didn't dare to look up, just in case no one was playing it!! But it was OK, it was just the 'worship crew' starting up again.

He looked up and saw Carol next to him singing.

'Strange,' he thought. 'I've hardly thought about her, and yet when I first got here she was all I could think about.' He noticed then how nice her voice was, how sparkly her eyes were ... in fact they were shining so much — she could have almost been tearful.

Which in fact was the case. The message that Bob had thought had been preached just for him, had also affected Carol in a big way as she realised how far away from Jesus she had let herself become.

When the service was over, Mrs. Ellis came up to Bob and asked him if he had enjoyed it.

"I hope it wasn't too much for you all at once!" she said.

"Well, it was a lot to take in, but I think I managed," he replied.

Mrs. Ellis had been watching him during the service and had seen the look on his face from time to time. She felt full up with sympathy for this boy from a hard background and wanted to try and help him all she could. "Have you got Sunday lunch waiting, or would you like to come back with us?" she asked.

Bob thought of the 'Sunday lunch' of corned beef and fried potatoes he had to get ready for his dad and knew that the Ellises were bound to be having a proper roast dinner. Perhaps he could phone his dad and explain ... no, it wouldn't be fair — especially now he had become a Christian.

"Thanks a lot, but I have to cook for dad as well," he said.

"Well, I'm sure we would have room for your dad too," smiled Mrs. Ellis.

"No, it's OK," he said. He knew that his dad would have had a few by now, and he wasn't taking him round to Terry's drunk.

Terry came over. He had been chatting to some of the other young people there. Carol was with him and they looked as if they were ready to go. "Coming home then?" asked Terry, his jacket hanging over his shoulder. "Me and Carol are going your way."

"Yeh, right." He went back to his seat where he had left his jacket and was immediately pounced upon by more kids who wanted to know who he was and if he was coming again next week. He managed to untangle himself from them and came back over to Terry and Carol.

"Right," said Terry. "Let's go."

"Hey, Terry!" called a voice.

They turned round. It was Alan, the minister.

"Could you spare a few minutes to talk about next week's youth meeting?" he asked.

Terry frowned. He didn't mind, but he wanted to walk home with Bob and find out how he felt about the service and everything. Alan would keep him talking for at least fifteen minutes.

He turned round to Bob and Carol.

"You go on ahead and I'll try and catch you up, all right?" he said.

Bob and Carol both nodded. Oh boy, this was an awkward one. It was just what Bob wanted, and yet now he felt almost shy about it. I mean, it's OK if you just chat someone up, but this was a bit different.

They started off down the road in silence, both of them trying to think of something to say that wouldn't sound like a leading question or anything. In the end Bob said, "It's nice, your church. Have you always gone to it?"

Carol looked at the pavement. "Well I used to go a lot, when I was younger but I haven't been so much lately, and then when you and Terry were in that fire ..."

"Oh," he butted in. "I thought you were a Christian like Terry."

"I am!" she flashed back, and then steadied herself. "Well, I haven't kept it up as well as Terry. There were things that put me off and so I didn't go any more."

"Like what?" Bob was intrigued by this conversation. Carol was so easy to talk to.

Carol sighed. "Oh, I don't know. People looking down at you in church if you come dressed a bit different, and the pressure you get to go to every single meeting. I mean, like Terry's Christian Union. Just because you're a Christian doesn't mean you have to go to everything with a Christian label on it, does it?"

Bob thought about this. "So it's not got nothing to do with Jesus, then, these reasons why you don't always go to church?"

She shook her head. "No. That's the trouble really. Giving your life to Jesus is great but it's some of the trimmings that get up my nose."

"Why don't you just tell them to … no, I don't suppose you can, really, can you? Personally, I'm not going to take any notice of what anyone else says. I mean, your vicar put it well when he said, 'If Jesus tells you to do it — do it.' That seems to be the best way." He rambled on for a while about what he was and wasn't going to do and didn't realise that Carol was looking at him in astonishment.

"Bob," she said. "Do you really mean that? Have you really become a Christian?"

Bob shrugged his shoulders. "Yeh, I suppose so. I mean, I don't know the half of it yet but as far as giving your life over goes — I did that this morning. Here, Carol …"

"What?"

"I don't suppose you'd come out with me tomorrow night? I mean, just to chat. We could go to that new burger bar, you're real easy to talk to, did you know that?"

The only thing Carol knew was that Bob had just asked her out and she was waiting for him to finish speaking so she could say yes! She was trying hard to smooth her gold hair and make herself look a bit more attractive … oh, come on, Bob, shut up for goodness sake!!

"All right then," she said. "Where shall I meet you?"

Bob couldn't believe it! It had been so easy!

"Er … howabout the clock tower in town? Half past seven."

"OK. Oh, this is my turning, see you tomorrow

then?" She smiled and flew down her road before he could see the look on her face.

11

Meet You at the Clock Tower

"Carol ... you don't like cornflakes," said Terry. He had been sitting observing his sister over the breakfast table, and he couldn't make out what was going on. She had been unusually quiet last night, and even when Sharon had phoned she just told him to tell her that she would see her at school today. Now she was pouring cornflakes into her bowl!

Carol looked up startled. "Pardon? What?"

"I said, 'You don't like cornflakes'," repeated Terry.

Carol frowned, puzzled at this silly statement from her brother.

"I know I don't! What are you telling me for?" she asked.

"Because you're pouring them into your bowl and all over the table. That's why!" he said.

Carol jumped as she saw the packet in her hand, and quickly put it back on the tablecloth. "Rats!" was all she said, and helped herself to coffee.

This exclamation didn't really satisfy Terry's curiosity. There was something strange going on. Even before the cornflake saga there had been the fact that she had been singing in the bathroom (she *never* did that), then she had smiled at everyone and been thoroughly pleasant to everyone — which was unheard of at this time in the morning. The other factor was that she was up in time for school!

"Are you OK?" he ventured.

Carol continued making her coffee and avoided looking at him.

"Of course I'm all right. Why shouldn't I be?" she said.

That did it. Terry put his cup down.

"All right. What's happened?" he said.

She looked at him blankly.

"Carol, I am your brother. I know you better than anyone else on earth, so don't try to kid me." Then a thought struck him. "Hey! It wouldn't be anything to do with Bob, would it?"

By way of an answer Carol blushed like a Belisha beacon.

Terry leaned back in his chair. "OK, from the beginning."

Actually, Carol was pretty relieved to tell someone that Bob had asked her out; she was bursting to tell Sharon but hadn't wanted to say anything on the phone. So she told Terry what had happened when they walked home, how Bob had talked seriously about being a Christian and how he had admired Carol for being easy to talk to and how it all led to Bob asking her out.

Before Terry could answer, Mrs. Ellis came in with Carol's schoolbag. "Carol, love, you left this in the bathroom! I don't think it will help you much at school there, do you? Anyway, it's time you weren't here."

And with that she hustled them both from the table.

"I'll see you later at school, all right?" Terry shouted to Carol as he made his way out of the front door.

Carol stood staring at the wallpaper. "Eh? What? Oh, yeh, OK."

Mrs. Ellis stood in the doorway holding the empty coffee mugs.

"Really, Carol, your grammar is terrible!"

・ ・ ・ ・ ・

Terry walked to school alone with his thoughts. He was very preoccupied with what Carol had said, and he didn't really know how he felt about it all. Obviously, he was ecstatic that Bob had been so enthusiastic about his church, and that he had in fact prayed to ask Jesus into his life ... that was what he himself had been praying for. It had been a long and exhausting weekend and yet the end results had been more than he could possibly hope for.

So why did he feel unsettled?

"Lord, there are times when I don't understand myself," he prayed as he walked along. "I mean, this was what my whole prayer life has been about just lately — and now it's all happened! Bob has become a Christian — and I don't expect him to turn into an angel overnight. He'll need a lot of help and it's great that he's asked Carol to help him ... I think. Oh I don't know, maybe I'm just jealous because I've done all the hard work and now Carol is taking over." He was nearly at the school gates now and he could see Martin in the distance waiting for him. But there was something else bothering him, and he had to confess it ... now! "OK, Lord! I know this is going to sound really mean, but the truth of the matter is that although Bob is a Christian, and he's really making an effort to try and do things differently — I don't want him going out with my sister! There! That's the truth out! I don't think he's good enough for her, and maybe all my efforts to get him converted were done from the wrong angle. I've treated him like a lost puppy — just like my mum said ... only now, I don't know what to do with him."

Martin came running up grinning and shouted, "Hey, Terry! Come on, I want to know all the details. What did the police say? Have you got to go to court or what?"

Terry shot him a glance that shut him up in midstream.

"Not now, Martin, I'm not in the mood," he said.

Martin took a step back. This was not like Terry at all! He never got moody — what on earth's happened?

They walked silently into school together, with Martin feeling terribly guilty for no reason at all. He decided to try again.

"Terry, is everything all right? You look worried," he said.

"That's the silly thing, everything is brilliant — it couldn't be better." He looked at his friend. "Bob Harris became a Christian last night." And before Martin had time to react, the bell went and hordes of kids came tearing down the corridors, obliterating any conversation.

"See you at break!" shouted Terry as he joined the chaotic mob.

Poor old Martin — it was such a long time till break before he could find out what had happened to Terry. He managed to have a quick chat with Helen and explained to her how his friend had reacted.

"Hmm," said Helen. "Perhaps we should all meet at break, you know, you and I and Peter and Simon and everyone. It sounds to me like he could do with a good chat and some sound advice!"

Martin looked worried. "I don't know if we're up to dishing out advice, Helen. I mean, Terry is after all the *leader* of the C.U."

"That doesn't mean he doesn't need us at times," she said. "We'll meet at our usual table — oh, and Martin, try and be a bit subtle with him, hmm?"

So when break arrived there was suddenly a wealth of Christians all sitting round one table with Terry looking panic stricken in the middle.

"What's all this?" he asked, looking round at them all.

"Terry," said Helen, "we only want to help. Perhaps you could start by telling us about the fire — everyone's heard about it!"

"Yeh!" said Martin. "What was the fine?" Helen dug him hard in the ribs.

"Aggh!" he exclaimed.

Terry resigned himself to the fact that they had to know some time.

"Well, I guess you're entitled to some explanations seeing as I have asked for your support and prayers. So, to answer Martin's question, we got what was generally known as a Verbal Caution. That means that you go down to the station with your parents and the police give you a right telling off in front of everyone and it's very very embarrassing. They told us that we were lucky we didn't get charged with Criminal Damage, but they believed it was an accident."

The C.U. were all ears, leaning forward on the table so that it kept toppling to one side.

"What's this about Bob Harris?" asked one of the others. "We heard he went to your church on Sunday, someone saw him coming out with your sister."

Terry looked pained for a moment and then said, "Yes, you're quite right, Bob went to my church on Sunday. He has in fact confessed that he needs Jesus in his life and I want you all to give him as much encouragement as you can, OK? Don't overdo it, but don't ignore it either, understand?"

There was much discussion amongst the group after this piece of news and Terry managed to get away while they were still talking.

"Hey, Helen," said Simon. "What's with Terry? I thought he'd be over the moon about Bob, but he looks like he's just lost a fiver!"

Helen gave him a knowing look and said, "Yes, there's something not quite right about all this."

Meanwhile Terry had managed to find his sister with her friends and called her over to one side.

"Carol, can I speak to you for a minute?" he said.

Carol was all giggles and excitement and had obviously been giving her friends the lowdown. "Sure, Tell. See you later, ladies!" she shouted as they walked off down the corridor.

Carol turned to Terry. "Right. What's so urgent?" she asked.

"Nothing. I just fancied a chat, that's all. Are you seeing Bob tonight then?" He tried to ask cautiously, but it didn't really work.

"You know I am," she replied, looking surprised. "Why?"

Her brother was silent.

"Hey, Terry! What's the matter?" she frowned.

He shoved his hands deep into his pockets ... "Carol, do you think it's a wise thing to do?" he asked.

"What are you talking about? It was *you* who introduced me to Bob in the first place!" Carol was getting upset.

"Yes, yes, I know. But at the time I didn't realise that he liked you. I mean, he's only been a Christian five minutes and he's a very rough character ..." he said.

Carol exploded. "Now you listen to me, Terry! If you are so set on seeing people become Christians then you have got to start taking chances! Bob has asked me out tonight and we were going to have a further chat about being a Christian as well as just having a nice time — but if you are going to try and put him down before he's had a chance to change — well there's one thing I can tell you! When we walked home on Sunday morning, Bob asked me why I didn't go to church more often, and I told him it was because people didn't give you a chance ... they criticised all the time and that's just what you're doing now! People like you are the reason people like Bob don't go back to church the next week!" And with that mouthful she flounced off back to her mates.

Terry was stunned! His sister had never been so nasty to him and looking back he decided that he had deserved that thunderbolt. Perhaps Carol and Bob would be good for each other ... perhaps ... why was all this happening? He was having such a hard time and yet he was only trying to do good! "Oh I give up!" he said out loud, and walked round the corner and bumped straight into Mr. Bellamy.

"Aah! It's our self-righteous Mr. Ellis! Well, boy, you have been having fun lately, haven't you? Got yourself into the local paper this afternoon. What was it it said? 'Thugs set fire to house.' This won't do your image any good, will it, Ellis? You are about to take a dive, boy, and I will be there to watch you fall! Got it? Now, back to your class, Ellis, back to your class."

Terry was very relieved to get home from school on that Monday. He felt it had been the worst day of his life. Everything he had done had gone wrong, and now he needed to see Carol and apologise for his behaviour towards her and Bob.

"That you, Terry?" called Mrs. Ellis from the kitchen.

"Yes, I'm home. Is Carol back yet?" he shouted from the hall.

"She's upstairs." His mum appeared, wiping her hands. "It's funny, she's in a bit of a strange mood. I thought she was meeting Bob tonight — but she certainly doesn't look like someone who's excited about a date!"

Terry ran upstairs to his sister's room and knocked on the door.

"Who is it?" came the muffled reply.

"It's me," he stated. For a moment he thought she was going to tell him to go away. Then the door opened and Carol let him in. She sat on her bed and looked at him expectantly.

"I'm sorry about today, Cas. No excuses. I was wrong to pull Bob to bits like that — I hope you have a really great night out." Terry waited for her reaction and prayed she would understand his side of things.

She picked at the fluff on her duvet cover for a while

and then said, "That's all right. Maybe it was good timing really. I mean, Bob and I feel the same way about people and it's good that I've chatted to you about it. We both need some guidance really but I think it's important that we get to know each other." She looked up at her brother. "Give us a breathing space, eh?"

"Sure," he said and left the room.

．　．　．　．　．

"Oh I remember her ... the one that brought us the tea when we were round Terry's house." Mr. Harris was hearing about Bob's date. He was pleased that Bob had found a nice girl. Maybe that was what he needed more than anything. He had also heard about the church service yesterday and that hadn't sounded too bad either.

"I'm taking her to the burger bar in town, so I won't want much to eat before I go out," said Bob.

"You mean you're too nervous to eat! I remember the first time I took your mother out ..."

The room went very quiet and Bob looked stony.

"Yeh, well, anyway," said his dad trying to cover up the atmosphere.

Bob picked up some dirty cups and took them into the kitchen. He couldn't stand hearing his dad talk about his mum. Even though it was a long time ago now, it still hurt to remember her and the way he loved her. How *could* she have left them like that?

He threw the cups into the sink and went to his room.

．　．　．　．　．

Carol was ready ages before time. She had changed her outfit four times, from a posh dress that would give the wrong impression to her worst jeans that probably did the same. Then she tried on the skirt she'd bought last week and finally settled for some better jeans and her new long jacket ... after all, they were only going to the burger bar! Trying to think of ways to make the time go faster, she decided to phone Sharon.

"Sharon?"

"Oh, hello, Carol! I didn't expect you to phone to-night ... thought you'd be too busy!" said her friend.

"You're joking. I've changed four times already! Sharon, talk to me, I need someone to calm my nerves!"

"Don't be stupid! Good grief, it's not as if it's your first date! How do you feel anyway?" she asked.

"Very nervous. I don't really know why. I don't suppose I've ever been out with anyone like Bob before. I don't know how to act or anything," worried Carol.

"Just be yourself! Oh, come on, Carol, you can handle this! Where are you meeting him?"

"I'm not telling you! I don't want you hiding round the corner watching!" she said.

"As if I would!" retorted Sharon, and then they both laughed at the thought. "Listen, Carol, I've got to go, my dad wants to use the phone. I'll see you tomorrow, all right? Bye!"

"Bye, Shaz," said Carol and placed the phone back on the receiver.

All of a sudden it was time to go and Carol had one last look at herself in a full length mirror (they always tell you to do that in magazines) and she left for town.

It was pretty cold outside and Carol was pleased she had chosen her long jacket; it looked nice and it was warm as well. As she turned the corner she could see the clock tower. Bob wasn't there yet and so she walked very slowly towards it. Her stomach was doing somersaults and she tried breathing deeply to get rid of the nerves. She looked at her watch. As it was only 7.20 she was ten minutes early, so she decided to go and look in some shop windows for a while and at the same time she could keep her eye on the clock tower for Bob appearing.

From the windows she could see the reflection of the tower and it was now 7.35 and Bob still wasn't there. Perhaps he was waiting around as well! Carol walked over and sat down on the bench under the clock. She looked around. Town was virtually deserted. It seemed like everyone had gone to wherever they were going. She looked at her watch again ... 7.45. He was now definitely late! Should she be cross with him or just brush it aside? No, she didn't want to start out on the wrong footing, so she would just smile and say, 'That's OK, I've only just got here myself!'

By 8.15 she felt awful. There was no sign of Bob, and she had been giving him 'five more minutes' for ages. 'Nobody is three quarters of an hour late for a first date!' she told herself. 'He's not coming, Carol, you might as well go home.' But she didn't. She hung around until nine o'clock and then she gave up and went home in tears.

When she reached the house, she let herself in with her key as quietly as she could so that she could reach her room and have a good howl before Terry knew she was in — it was a bit of luck for her that her mum and dad were out till late.

But she couldn't escape ... she met Terry on the landing. Immediately she put her head down to hide her face.

"Hi, Carol, you're home early! How did it go!" he said cheerfully.

There was no reply, and Carol tried to brush past him but he caught hold of her arm.

"Just a minute! Hey, you've been crying! Carol! What happened??" he yelled.

She faced him, tears streaming down her face … "Leave me alone!!"

12

How Do You Feel?

Terry was thrown into utter confusion, seeing Carol like that, and unfortunately he jumped to the ultimate wrong conclusion.

'How dare he??' he raged. 'I *knew* he was no good! After all I tried to do for him! I'll kill him!'

He battered on Carol's door ... "Cas! Let me in!" he yelled. And she did, mainly because Terry sounded like he was about to let the whole street in on her affairs. He rushed in the room and caught hold of her shoulders.

"What did he do? Come on, Carol, where is he? I'll murder him!" he said, still shaking with rage at what he thought had happened. All of a sudden there was too much shouting going on as Carol tried to shout him down to say what had really happened and Terry kept flying off the handle about what he'd do to Bob Harris, that for a while neither of them listened to what the other one was saying. Then Carol picked up a pile of books and held them high above her head and threw them on the floor. They came crashing down and stunned them both to silence.

"OK," said Carol calmly. "Now listen. Bob didn't try anything, Bob didn't do anything because Bob *didn't turn up!"*

Terry stood there breathing very heavily and trying to take in what Carol had just said.

"He what?" he asked blankly.

"Terry, Bob didn't turn up." It was a bald statement made without emotion. She was tired and fed up and wanted to be on her own. Terry immediately felt embarrassed and guilty for a hundred and fifty different reasons. He put his arm round his sister.

"Oh Carol, I'm sorry. Perhaps he was held up or something," he said, trying to be helpful.

"Or perhaps he just didn't want to go out with me after all," said Carol, feeling tearful all over again.

Terry didn't really know what was the best move to make next, so he said, "Look, you sit here and I'll go and make you some coffee, all right?" Carol was grateful to her brother, one, because she really needed the coffee and two, because it gave her a chance to cry in private before he came back again. What a pig that Bob was! Fancy doing that to her ... he had seemed to really care and be interested about her, and they had so much in common. She sighed, 'I really thought he would be a help to me too!' She had thought quite a bit about their conversation on the way home from church yesterday and she had even hoped that perhaps between the two of them they could give Christianity a face-lift amongst some of their mates ....

The door opened and Terry came in with two steaming mugs of coffee. They sat and talked for a while, and he gradually got her to laugh politely at his jokes. Then, just as she was coming round a bit, the front doorbell rang. Carol stiffened.

"Don't worry, I'll get it," said Terry, already up. "If

it's Sharon, do you want to see her or not?"

"I don't want to see anybody," she said dully.

Terry went downstairs and answered the door.

It was Bob.

He just stood there, and Terry was unable to decide how to act, so they both stood there for a while. Then Terry said, "Well?"

Bob shifted from one leg to the other. "I've come to see Carol." He looked terribly guilty and upset.

"She doesn't want to see anyone ... least of all you," he replied quietly.

"Look," said Bob. "I have to see her, really. You see I didn't turn up tonight and I want to explain."

"I think you've done enough damage for one night," Terry replied and went to shut the door. Two things happened at once. Bob put his foot in the door and Carol ran down the stairs. She had heard Bob's voice from her room and had to find out what was going on.

"It's all right, Terry, I'll talk to him," she said softly and so he left her at the door.

Bob felt very uncomfortable standing outside so he asked, "Is there any chance I can come in and talk to you on your own for a minute?"

Carol thought about it and said, "All right, come in the kitchen. I'll make a drink."

He heaved a sigh of relief and followed her through.

They sat at either side of the large kitchen table peering at each other through the steam of their drinks. Carol had the feeling that everything was going to turn out all right, although she still didn't know what had happened to him tonight.

Bob grinned. "Not quite the burger bar is it?" he said, breaking the ice.

She laughed and shook her head.

"I'd better tell you what happened, hadn't I?" he said.

"That would be nice," replied Carol, trying to sound cross and failing miserably.

His expression changed as he tried to explain. "You see, such a lot has been happening to me over the last couple of weeks that all of a sudden, I couldn't cope with it. I mean, my dad has gone from being a real drunken slob who couldn't give me the time of day — to a real drunken slob who cares about me!"

Carol laughed again.

He went on ... "I've been introduced to Jesus through Terry — and I've been nicked by the police twice!" At this point he joined in laughing. "It's all insane, isn't it? And then of course there was this girl I fancied but I couldn't talk to in case her brother thought I was just using him to get to her! Then the next minute I've asked her out and we seem to have a lot in common and I can't wait to see her again ... and ..."

"And what?" Carol was sitting with her hands under her chin looking at him quizzically — she didn't know what a pretty picture it made.

"Well, Carol, how on earth can you be interested in someone like me? I am trying to be a Christian. I've got such a lot to learn and I'm going to need a lot of help. I'm sure I will be a right pain — are you sure you can cope with it all?" He put *his* hands under his chin and looked back at her.

Carol thought again, put her head on one side and replied. "I don't suppose it occurred to you for a moment that I might need help too? Bob, we're both in the same boat! We're both trying our best to make our faith work so what better way than to join forces?"

Bob reached out for Carol's hand.

"You really want to try?" he asked.

"Yeh," she said.

The door opened suddenly and they both jumped about four feet in the air.

It was Terry.

"I'm sorry, I know I shouldn't barge in but I had to make sure Carol was all right." By now he could see she was — but it was a bit late to do anything else but stand there like a twit.

Bob and Carol looked at each other and laughed.

"Yeh, Terry, she's all right! Come in and join us. Carol was just going to make some more coffee and I wanted to ask you a few things about this Christian Union of yours. You know, I thought, maybe if we could get hold of some decent Christian videos — do they exist? Right! Well, get some of those and go round the school ...."

PRAYING WITH JESUS
Dr. Paul Y. Cho

Prayer is a dialogue with God in which our attitudes and thoughts are grafted into God's thoughts.

In *Praying with Jesus* the author takes us deep into the teaching of the Lord's Prayer. This is the perfect model for our own prayers but more than that, it shows us how to align our thoughts with God's purposes for the world and for His people.

For prayer to be accomplished our thoughts on God must be right, and this is where the book begins. Dr. Cho then takes us phrase by phrase through the rest of the Lord's Prayer. He writes not only with theological insight, but as a pastor who has seen these principles working out in people's lives over the years.

If you want to receive clearer answers to your prayers, if you simply want to draw nearer to God, then try *Praying with Jesus*.

Catalogue Number YB 9165   £2.50

PRAYER: KEY TO REVIVAL
Dr. Paul Y. Cho

Published in March 1985 and reprinted six times in the same year, this best-selling title has now been reissued with a 32 page study guide. Dr. Cho says, 'It is because I believe in revival and renewal that I have written this book. It has been historically true that prayer has been the key to every revival in the history of Christianity.'

From his experience as a pastor, Dr. Cho answers general questions such as *why* to pray and *when* to pray. He also deals with specific queries like, 'What does prayer accomplish?' 'What part does the Holy Spirit play in prayer?' and 'Why does fasting increase the effectiveness of prayer?'

His study is based on one simple premise: 'God has no favourite children . . . If God has worked through men and women in the past, He can work through you.'

'This is the best book I have ever read on prayer.'
EVANGELISM TODAY

DR. PAUL CHO, who was converted from Buddhism as a young man, is now Pastor of the Central Church in Seoul, which has grown to over half a million members. He is also founder of Church Growth International.

Catalogue Number YB 9059   £2.75

MORE THAN NUMBERS
Dr. Paul Y. Cho

No one is better qualified to speak out on the sometimes misunderstood church growth movement than Dr. Cho. A pastor with over thirty years' experience, he now leads a church in Seoul, Korea, which currently has over a million members. He writes, however, that 'Success has not come quickly or easily. Most of the lessons I have learned have come as a result of passing difficult tests in my life and ministry.'

Dr. Cho writes with a theological sensitivity which enables him to base church growth on a solid spiritual foundation instead of mere technique, discussing such diverse topics as revival, the cell system, the media and the Kingdom of God.

'Word Books have done the church a service by reissuing this excellent book by Dr. Cho. I regard it as vital reading on church growth. There is nothing stereotyped about Cho's teaching – he is a man of the Spirit and this comes through clearly.'
COLIN WHITTAKER, RENEWAL

Catalogue Number YB 9100   £2.25